# *Goose River Anthology, 2019*

*Edited by*

*Deborah J. Benner*

Goose River Press
Waldoboro, Maine

Library of Congress Card Number: 2019951667

ISBN: 978-1-59713-207-7 paperback
ISBN: 978-1-59713-208-4 hard cover

First Printing, 2019

Cover photo by Monica Tilley

Published by
***Goose River Press***
3400 Friendship Road
Waldoboro ME 04572
e-mail: gooseriverpress@roadrunner.com
www.gooseriverpress.com

## *Authors Included*

## *Authors Included*

*In Memory*
*of those who fought*
*for our freedom.*

*Special thanks to Sue Campagna for her*
*wonderful help in proofing the book.*

**Ilga Winicov Harrington**
**Falmouth, ME**

## The Ghost of Papa Doc

The Haiti airport near Port au Prince is sweltering hot and noisy. Sweat is running down my back. I'm pushing my hair out of my eyes with one hand while the other is clutching the telephone to my ear. At least the phone is ringing. It rings and rings and rings, but I will not give up hoping that someone at the other end will pick it up. And then, they finally do.

"Hello," *where have I heard that strange voice before?*

"Is this the Oloffson Hotel?" I ask.

"Yes, *madame,*" the voice answers with an insinuating lilt and I suddenly recognize the unmistakable voice of Monsieur Jolicoeur. He is the self-proclaimed "Director of Tourism" and informant to the Haitian secret police, all rolled in one dapper little man. In his white suit and Panama hat, with his photographic memory, he meets every incoming airplane and keeps track of each foreigner while in Haiti. He had met our incoming plane a week ago and had been offensively "attentive" to me on our first evening in the hotel.

"This is Mrs. Winicov calling from the airport. We can't leave for St. Tomas this afternoon, since no planes leave till after the president's funeral tomorrow. My husband and I want to know if you still have our reservation for tonight?" I make a pointed reference to my husband to remind him that I'm not traveling alone. But he would remember, naturally!

"Of course, *madame,*" his voice continues to ooze on the phone, "we are *expecting you,*" His words slide across the wires and I think of all the Nazi war movies I had seen. There is a dull crash at the other end of the phone and he hangs up. Despite the heat, I shiver.

I take a deep breath, turn to my husband and explain the latest wrinkle in this incredible day that started before dawn ninety miles away at the Mellon Clinic, where we had spent

**Ilga Winicov Harrington**
**Falmouth, ME**

the week of April 1971 with our friends in Haiti.

***

We had been visiting our friend, her husband Chad and infant-daughter. Chad, a Quaker physician, was working two years in Haiti to fulfill his "alternative service" to the military during the Vietnam War. Our previous exchange of letters had made us aware of Papa Doc Duvalier's dictatorship and instability of the country and we had made this Caribbean trip without our boys, even though they had loved the sunny climes on previous trips. It was turning out to be a wise decision!

We had not been prepared for the abject poverty of the country, the lack of sanitation, medical care and most of the things we take for granted at home. We did see incredible waterfalls, places of natural beauty and found phenomenally skilled artists in wood carving and textiles. But much of the country was denuded of trees for firewood and there were no wild animals on the island. They had all been eaten. That is, if you did not count the rats.

In the midst of this, medical care was almost non-existent outside the capital, except at the Mellon Clinic. There the doctors and staff were faced not only with child malnutrition but also local practices and superstitions, such as rubbing the newborns umbilical cord in the fireplace ashes, which often led to tetanus and infant death. My friend Joan told of delivering her daughter at the Clinic Hospital and being forced to leave the room in a couple of hours after the birth for a critical surgery patient. The monumental amount of care provided despite lack of facilities and personnel was starkly demonstrated as I accompanied Chad on his clinic rounds in the courtyard of the hospital one morning.

The sun baked courtyard overflowed with human misery and stench as patients and families waited their turn. The women squatted as plucked flowers in their colorful skirts

**Ilga Winicov Harrington**
**Falmouth, ME**

with patient, tired faces. A mother nursed her baby with another child clutching her skirt. A man with a bloody cloth around his arm was leaning against a wall next to an old man who squatted scowling, puffing on a pipe. Chad and I made the rounds, with his local assistant, who translated the Creole French spoken by patients and their families. Only those with severe trauma were admitted inside the clinic, the rest were given treatment or medications right in the court-yard while the rest if the patients dozed or watched. But this was the best anyone could do 90 miles away from the capi-tal.

Before first light this morning there had been loud knocks at our friend's cottage door. We heard Chad answer and after a moment he called for my husband. As we all breathlessly gathered at the front door we saw the gray-haired man from the clinic staff, who briskly informed us of the momentous news that Papa Doc Duvalier had died and there was a general curfew on the island. The clinic was far enough away from Port au Prince, so that any unrest was immediately unlikely, but suddenly everyone realized that we had a serious problem.

We had planned to leave for the city that afternoon, stay at Oloffson's Hotel overnight and take an early flight next morning to St Thomas for a few additional days of vacation. In rapid consultation with several of the local staff, we were strongly advised to go to the airport right away and try to get an immediate flight, before riots and political clashes made leaving an impossibility. We packed in a mad rush, my friend Joan gathered us some breakfast and fruit to take along, since no one was willing to predict how easy it would be to get to the airport, which was on the way to Port au Prince.

There was serious apprehension about the trip we were about to make today. Even under normal conditions and with the car bearing the clinic logo, random checkpoints on the roads with gun toting local militias collected bribes for a safe passage note, sometimes written on a gum wrapper, to proceed. We said a silent prayer and hugged each other with promises to meet again in Philadelphia in a year's time. The sun was just peeking over the horizon, as we left through the clinic gates, beautifully illuminating the brilliant reds and purples of bougainvillea and hibiscus of this place of both misery and hope.

We traveled in silence along the road, weaving here and there to avoid the potholes accumulated from decades of neglect since the road was built. Surprisingly, we only encountered one checkpoint and the interaction with the militia was quick and non-confrontational. However, our driver returned worried with our pass. Apparently, everyone in surroundings was getting ready to go to Port au Prince, with demonstrations and the funeral held tomorrow at noon. Just before the airport he stopped at a gas station for additional information gathering. More bad news! All outgoing flights were cancelled. The driver would take us no further than the airport and definitely not to Port au Prince, since roaming armed gangs were confiscating cars at gunpoint. At the airport he dropped us off and left quickly. As he unloaded our bags he muttered.

"Surely hope to make it back to the clinic, without having to run anyone down to get there."

"*Bonne chance!*" and he left.

***

The scene at the airport is hectic. A plane has arrived with international news and camera crews, but true to our driver's information, all flights leaving Haiti have been suspended until after the funeral. We manage to book a flight on the first plane out to St. Thomas tomorrow afternoon. There are reports of unrest already in Port au Prince and we are told that all military personnel have been mobilized. The Question of "who is running the country, town and all the usual establishments" has become increasingly more problematic, especially in view of my conversation with Monsieur Jolicoeur.

Miraculously we find a taxi willing to take us to Oloffson's for an exorbitant price. The curfew makes the city less crowded, but absence of the milling crowds makes the presence of the armed special operations Tonton Macoutes more threatening. These feared men are now everywhere. There is a cordon of police around Oloffson's, but we are allowed to pass and soon we are up the front steps and are standing at the reception desk. The dark paneled lobby with potted plants and the open veranda windows offers a cool oasis from the heat and the bright sun. It probably has not changed since Graham Greene took notes for *The Comedians*" there years ago. The desk clerk checks us in, gives us room keys and the additional warning not to leave the hotel grounds. Only the press may roam the city and even they have to be accompanied by two armed guards. We have landed in probably the safest place in Port au Prince, the official bastion of the World Press, here for the funeral of Papa Doc.

The hotel is almost eerie. On our first night in Haiti, before going out to the clinic, the lobby and the dining room had been crowded with noise and laughter everywhere. That time we were lodged in the old part of the hotel, which had previously been the "bishop's residence." It was built around a romantic courtyard with a walkway for the second-floor rooms overlooking the garden below. Our room on the second floor closed with wooden louvered door that permitted a cross breeze with the outside window and allowed you to listen to the gurgling fountain below as you fell asleep. Now our room is in the more modern Annex, where television cables are stretched along the walkways in front of the rooms and the sound of generators is almost deafening.

The press must have been busy chasing down stories all evening, since we are almost the only diners in the dining room. Almost, but not quite. In his inimitable and almost invisible manner, Monsieur Jolicoeur appears from behind

**Ilga Winicov Harrington**
**Falmouth, ME**

one of the potted palms some time during dinner, greets us and bends over to kiss my hand: "*Enchanté, Madame.*" His manners remain impeccable even in crisis, but fortunately he is too busy to linger.

The dining room remains quiet with impeccable service and only soft music provided by the man at the grand piano in the corner of the lobby. We seem cocooned in an incongruous oasis in the midst of occasional shouts and sporadic gunfire in the distance. The air seems thick with unnamed threats and the soft tinkling piano sound becomes almost otherworldly. We do not linger long over coffee after dinner amidst the potted palms, but retreat to our room. The sound of all-night generators only adds to our anxiety over the next steps in our journey tomorrow.

Next morning passes slowly, as we are confined to the hotel. We try to arrange our return to the airport as early as possible, but the hotel clerk tells us phones are down, he hopes temporarily. We need to wait until early afternoon. We hear crowds and the parade in the distance, but the hotel remains empty except for a few staff at the desk and some security guards outside. When the taxi finally arrives in the afternoon, we had almost given up hope. The driver seems nervous and uses back alleys to get out of the city, since all the major streets are still clogged with agitated crowds, but we reach the airport without any further problems.

And then surprisingly our plane takes off almost on time and we watch with relief as it turns over the water away from Haiti. Before long we are over another island and the plane turns sharply to land in the steep bowl like airfield of St. Thomas.

"Well, that is a relief," breathes my husband. "Now for a few days of peace and quiet."

The large hotel complex gleams in the late afternoon sun among the palms. A light breeze sways the colorful bougainvillea branches along the path and we enter the resort reception. The young man at the desk takes a look at

**Ilga Winicov Harrington**
**Falmouth, ME**

my reservation papers, which state the building and the room number we are to occupy for the next few days. He looks again and frowns and shakes his head.

"I'm sorry madam, but that room is unavailable," he says.

"And why not?" Exasperation makes my voice sharp. This Caribbean trip is not turning out to be the relaxing vacation we had planned.

"As I said, I'm very sorry, but we'll find you another."

"Now, really, I specifically arranged for that corner room with a particularly nice view...." I never finish the sentence.

The young man shakes his head and emphatically interrupts me.

"Madam, a plane crashed in that corner room late last night on landing, fortunately no one was there," and he sighs.

"I will try and find you a nice room in another building, if only you will give me a few minutes" and his sigh is full of forbearance.

We sit down suddenly overwhelmed. Let him take his time. We could have been there, but for the cancelled flights we tried to take because of Papa Doc's funeral.

***

**Sylvia Little-Sweat**
**Wingate, NC**

## Piano

Percussive black and white Steinway keys—
Intoned on felt-hammered golden strings.
Arpeggios, chords, and ebony harmonies,
Nuanced melodies, raucous cacophony, hand
Over hand, high-flying fingers on trapeze.

**Sandy Conlon**
**Steamboat Springs, CO**

## His Heart

Faithful friend and brother
Loving husband, son, and father

We listened as long as we could
To the beatings of your heart

To ease your passing
From this world to another

As fear began to fall away
In the Night Watches imagined for you

Climbing in rugged mountains
Skiing in the winter snows

Fishing lakes and sparkling streams
Breathing in the summer air

And riding horses running free
Through fields of green and gold

Then resting by still waters
In nature's wondrous wild finding peace

So you must have known
When all else has passed away

In the heart steady and strong
Love alone remains.

**Bob Whitmire**
**Round Pond, ME**

## Your Bed

Tonight, finally, I will sleep in the bed
where you slept the last night that you slept.

Crying without sound, feet faltering, I approach
the door, see the bed, now made, where I found you.

I stop, breathe, stand just outside the room,
looking in at the pile of pillows with cartoon penguin

pillow cases we bought to please the grandkids
on their monthly sleepovers; the afghan

you bunched around your shoulders because
it wasn't long enough to reach your feet.

How did we wind up sleeping in separate beds
at opposite ends of the house? You said it was

your back, incompatible with the mattress we bought
three years ago. You said we couldn't afford to buy

a new one. Were you being diplomatic? I couldn't
afford to lose you—and now you've left another way.

I stumble into the room, throw myself onto
the bed, kick my way under the covers,

searching for your scent, only to find myself staring
into the unblinking eye of a scarf-wrapped penguin.

You always could make me laugh.

**Meg Weston**
**Camden, ME**

## Dreams Interrupted

i'm sick of this getting up
in the middle of the night
i need my uninterrupted night's sleep
so i can do my job where everyone
wants to put their problems in my hands
as if i can fix anything
i don't need that from you too
i don't know why i'm expected to be
empathetic or nurturing or even a good cook
just because i was born with an X instead of a Y
i never wanted to be a teacher or a nurse
and i wondered what in hell i would do with a college
degree
i never wanted to be a therapist, a psychologist
or even a doctor with all that tending to sickness
although i could get into the diagnosing giving
my opinion and especially the illegible handwriting
i don't need that from you so don't keep waking
me up in the night with your plaintive cry
making me grudgingly leave the comfort
of my dreams my blanket my pillow so that you
won't decide that inside is just as good as outside
after all that training i have to take you out and
all you do is munch on the grass and sniff
each of the dandelions gone to seed in the
garden and i watch you wander over to the
wisteria arbor that has fallen to the
ground and needs to be propped up
you sit down and i follow your gaze to
the heavens filled with stars
and i take a moment to

(continued)

**Meg Weston**
**Camden, ME**

inhale the scent of night
before i gather you
in my arms and
take you back
to bed.

***

**Robert B. Moreland**
**Pleasant Prairie, WI**

## End of the Beginning

He undresses after tumultuous day
leaves him jobless and short of hope. T-shirt,
shorts, walks to the great lake. Severance pay
pitiful, alone considers professional hurt,

expendable. Balmy moonless night, stone
jetty still sun warmed, sits cross-legged as the
stars pepper his known universe alone
with lake mirrored images as far as he can see.

Then he slips into the water, chilled at first
until it consumes him, head visible;
one with the dark lake. Eyes closed, the curses
are swept away. Peace enfolds his heart full.

As he finds his place in wave iced starlight,
a still small voice whispers it will be all right.

**Elmae Passineau**
**Weston, WI**

## The Old Neighborhood

Patty's house was there,
  across the street and three doors down,
  my favorite childhood friend

She who asked,
  when I was four and new to town
  and nearly hairless,
  are you a boy or a girl?

She whom I worried about
  because she wasn't a Catholic,
  and a nun at school said non-Catholics
  wouldn't go to heaven

She who skated with me,
  double-dated with me,
  and introduced me to gin and sour

Patty fell out of my life eventually—
  her house is gone, too,
  replaced with a parking lot,
  rows and rows of meters, blacktop,
  and painted yellow lines

**Gerry Di Gesu**
**Union, NJ**

## Babe

My heart felt as heavy as the dull gray clouds that hung before us in the distance. I dreaded this trip because I was afraid of what I would find at the end of our journey. Roger, my husband, drove silently, a look of grim resignation on his face. Our three children sensed our somber mood for they sat quietly in the back of the car.

The rear of the station wagon was loaded with odds and ends of household furnishings we had scrounged from our attic and cellar: dishes and pots, plastic tables, an ancient lamp. An old braided rug had been cleaned and was tied tightly to the top of the car. Not the nicest furnishings for a new home but the best we had to offer. The one new item was a color television set we had purchased that morning.

"She has to have a tv set, hon, what else is there for her to do?" Rod asked. "She's not living with anyone now so there's no one to talk to and no place to go. We have to buy it for her." I knew he was right. Babe, my mother-in-law, is a gift and I love her with all my heart and wanted her to have the tv. But I resented one more purchase which would push us further into debt.

A week earlier she had called to tell me she had found an apartment. It was located in senior citizen housing in the heart of the city and she was moving immediately.

She was so excited on the phone I had no idea what she had gotten herself into. An impulsive person, I prayed she hadn't done anything foolish she would regret.

When Babe retired seven years earlier, her Social Security allowance, her only income, was not enough to continue paying her rent. She had to give up her apartment and friends in the town where she had grown up and lived most of her life and move fifty miles to live with her daughter, husband and three young children. She helped doing house-

**Gerry Di Gesu**
**Union, NJ**

work and baby-sitting as my sister-in-law worked to pay extra bills. It was a difficult time for Babe. Used to running her own home, she now had to do things the way her daughter's family lived. The strain of living with the noise and problems of raising three children under seven years old had become more than she could cope with. She knew she was welcome to live with us but wanted to be independent and didn't want to leave the new friends she had made. Now seventy, she wanted to make a new home and life for herself and I prayed God would help her find the joy and happiness she so deserved.

A bed and dresser were her only possessions. A beautiful, caring person, she owned no other furniture since he had given all her household goods to friends when she moved in with her daughter. Now she had nothing and no money to buy what she needed. Her meager Social Security allowance would just about cover the rent and she was too proud to let us help her.

Babe's life had not been easy. Widowed at thirty-five with three small children to raise, she had existed on Social Security benefits. Later she moved to her parents' home and nursed them both through terminal illnesses. After their death, her sisters and brothers wanted the home sold, so she was forced to move again. Shortly after she had a first mastectomy. Five years later, a second mastectomy was performed. That was nineteen years ago.

"If you've got it, you've got it," she said, referring to the cancer that had invaded her body. "No sense complaining, it just wastes time. I guess this is the life the Lord has planned for me so I might as well go along with it."

Any extra penny she had she shared with family and stranger equally. She worked as a cashier at a small neighborhood supermarket and often came home upset over the bad luck one of her customers was enduring, determined to do something to help. She never mentioned her good deeds, but since we lived in the same neighborhood, people would

**Gerry Di Gesu**
**Union, NJ**

stop to tell me how generous she had been to them. One had been given Babe's new winter coat. "It was too small for my big tummy anyway," she grinned. The free turkey she received each year from her employer usually ended up on a neighbor's Thanksgiving table. Household furnishings often found their way into the home of a struggling, newly-married couple.

On her day off she worked diligently to make her small apartment shine. Most furnishings were second-hand since that's what she could afford, but her gift for brightening her home was always evident in colorful pictures or knickknacks obtained from garage sales. When she moved into a dank and dark first floor apartment behind an upholstery shop, I was devastated because it was all she could afford. I should have known better. In a few weeks fresh paint, starched curtains and her happy smile brought a glow to her new home. Everyone was welcome at Babe's home and most holidays were spent around a table covered with special treats she could ill afford. "I want to take good care of my stomach," she would laugh, patting her ample tummy. It didn't matter that she had used her weekly salary for this holiday feast, only that she could share it. She was a true disciple although she would never think of herself that way. And now she was alone. It was her choice but somehow it didn't seem fair.

We pulled off the highway and entered the city. My heart crumbled. Stores and tenements lining the street that led to her new home were vacant and boarded up. Litter covered the sidewalks and there was little sign of life in the neighborhood. It was what I feared. She was impulsive and had charged off, taking the first apartment she was able to afford in this dismal, dangerous part of the city.

Further down the main street, though, we entered a section of the city being upgraded through urban renewal. My spirits lifted when I saw smiling faces of shoppers as they walked along the sidewalk. They reflected pride in the color-

**Gerry Di Gesu**
**Union, NJ**

ful, newly renovated shops that bloomed among the vacant, dilapidated buildings.

Soon Babe's high-rise complex loomed ahead of us, its new facade glistening in the sun. We found a parking spot and started to unpack the car. The kids pulled at the boxes, eager to see Grandma's new home. I was not as eager. But the entrance foyer was painted a bright yellow with ivy and marigolds scattered in redwood planters. Colorful travel posters covered an entire wall from floor to ceiling. Maybe Babe had made a good choice after all. We stepped off the elevator and walked down a long hall. At last we reached #708. My hand trembled as I rang the bell. What was inside?

"Hi gang, come on in," smiled Babe as she hugged us. "Wait till you see my new home." Always cheerful and happy, her blue eyes sparkled as she led us into her sun-filled living room. "Isn't this the greatest place," she grinned. She showed us through the large, airy rooms furnished only with her bed, dresser and rocking chair. "This is one of the nicest apartments in the building. At night I have a great view of the city and river. And there's always something to watch across the street," she said, pointing to a new office complex. She was as happy as a child with a new toy. "And look at this electric range. I never used one before but I tried the oven to bake a layer cake for you," she beamed. "This is a brand new building and sparkling clean. Isn't it great?" I felt encouraged but somehow couldn't dismiss the bleak atmosphere of the empty apartment with its huge bare windows. We laid the worn rug on the living room floor, opened the beach chairs, arranged small plastic tables and set the large antiquated lamp in the corner.

In a sunny corner of her bedroom resting on top of a sturdy box was her collection of houseplants. Leave it to Babe. Her home was always crowded with a profusion of blooming African violets. If anyone discarded a pot of sick-looking ivy or any other worn-out plant, Babe took it home and resur-

**Gerry Di Gesu**
**Union, NJ**

rected it with her good humor. I chuckled, remembering the "garden" she had cultivated before she had to move.

She had lived in a first floor apartment at the back of a run-down building. It faced a large, dirty courtyard cluttered with large chunks of broken cement and glass. A row of dilapidated garages in danger of collapse provided a buffer between her home and the railroad tracks directly behind them. It was a freight line and the cars whizzing along churned up dirt and cinders which filled her yard. There wasn't a patch of green visible.

Never daunted, Babe brought home some large wooden bushel baskets from the supermarket, filled them with top-soil and peat moss and planted her garden. By mid-summer she had transformed this soot-covered expanse into an oasis filled with prized tomato plants and mounds of brilliant petunias and geraniums.

"Isn't this great," she cried, waltzing through the rooms. "I can't believe I'm so lucky. Look at all I have," she beamed, waving her arms expansively. I stared at her. To me, everything looked bleak and shabby. But I wasn't surprised. Throughout her life she always accepted what God planned without complaining. Tired from unpacking, we plopped onto the beach chairs to rest and enjoy her coffee and cake.

"Wait I have a surprise for you," she bubbled, popping into the bedroom, blonde curls bouncing. She returned triumphantly holding a huge, hand-lettered sign which read: "To Babe—we all love you because you're such a nice lady. Signed—your dancing class." Her "dancing class" was a group of friends who met once a week at the community center on the first floor of her building for bingo, lunch, or dancing. Babe loved to dance and was always showing them new dance steps. Next month they were having their first "senior prom." Rushing back to the bedroom, she came out waving a big American flag and wearing a high, black soldier's hat, props for her part as a toy soldier in a Busby Berkely type of review scheduled for the following week. How I envied her

**Gerry Di Gesu**
**Union, NJ**

energy and zest for life.

"My dancing class gave me a kitchen shower," she beamed. "With all the excitement of unpacking I almost forgot to tell you. Yesterday at our meeting they surprised me and I got boxes and bags of canned goods and paper supplies plus almost everything I need for my new kitchen. I won't have to go shopping for months!" She smiled proudly, displaying her fully-stocked kitchen shelves.

Babe's friends had responded to her wonderful personality with a generous outpouring of gifts they could hardly afford. Most were low income retirees with little or no pension and many required supplemental government assistance. They had cheerfully shared the little they possessed and I had resented buying her a television set. I never had felt so selfish and uncaring.

Finally, we cleaned up and it was time to leave. As we said goodbye, I kissed a happy woman, not a lonely one. I envied her. On the ride home, I felt relieved, but more than that—humble. I had been busy feeling sorry for myself. Our income was adequate but inflation and high medical bills ate up more of my husband's salary each month. We kept sinking further into debt and I was unwilling to admit we had to change our way of life and re-examine our values to adapt to the present economy. I felt cheated and wanted too much.

But once again, as so many other times in the years that I've known her, Babe restored perspective to my life by showing me what living and being happy is really all about.

**Laureen Haben, osf**
**Milwaukee, WI**

## Hunting for Ruffed Grouse

On a late September day
feeling more like August
with a splash of yellow leaves
in a mostly green forest
this North Woods was brighter than usual.

Through a forest of aspens
thin like broomsticks
in fleeting slivers of light
hunters looked for the elusive bird
the one called the "King of upland birds."

Stepping in heavy dew-soaked boots
through dense cave-like shade
through a claustrophobic grove of poplars
in places plainly marked for grouse-hunting
the gun-carrying men sought their prey.

Though they happily saw
a twittering collage of woodchuck
and thundering flushes of grouse
they left the "Grouse Hunting Capital of the World"
with no bird in the bag.

**Jacob Fricke**
**Belfast, ME**

## Lost Ocean

the fog coughed complacency, smoothed its cloth of smarm
        over the town's plain tables
dropcloth alike to painted shrines and the sky

it's hard to hold an edge against so much nothing, the way
        the grey festers
doubt, turning spruce and standing deadwood into

a memory, whiting out the graves into
a whispered emotion, every real presence in this blur
        merely

a mock-up idea; in this
oil-jam of light, the mansions wear the same jawline

as rumors, the corner market you seek
all wrong, a dream returned from childhood

askew; the cutting, passive roar beside you
could be the overpass, could be the laundry

all your fine ghosts as nothing, faces never really there—
you yourself a dream, a reverie, some mistaken idea

and at some compass point before you—so the story goes—
        the sea.

**The late E.O. Barsalou**
**Kittery Point, ME**

## Tides

Rushing, surging waters of the tide, Changing your
direction and levels with time.

Seafarers watch closely that they may be allowed,
To leave on your cold blue surface,
And leave their loved ones far behind.

May their vessels be kept worthy
For the sea shall show no mercy.

Until they and their vessels return to safe harbors.

Their holds will be filled with the long trip's catch.

The work is not over; they have damaged nets.

The work will continue during the changing of the tides.

When they leave again on your cold blue surface,
And leave their loved ones far-behind.

***

**Sally Belenardo**
**Branford, CT**

## Jet and Contrail

Sun-reflecting bird
streaks across sky, leaves behind
its white excrement.

**Gerald George**
**Belfast, ME**

## Was Something Wrong?

She watched them drag her parents into the street,
made them take old toothbrushes to the grime
embedded in the stones by thousands of shoes,
then threw rocks through windows,
shattering the glass.
At first they didn't notice her standing there,
wondering what her family had done.

Was something wrong with how they'd baked the bread?
Had the fruit gone bad? Had some patron complained?
Had someone been short-changed?
If only the customer had told them what was wrong.
Why force her parents out?
What would warrant such mean treatment
as cleaning the old street?

Angry tears appeared upon her face.
This little place had been her only home,
full of comforting smells, where every day,
when school let out, she helped to keep the shop.
She ran outside, crying for her parents.
A uniformed guard quick-lifted his rifle-butt.
She never saw it coming.

**Rosemary Sedgwick**
**Boxborough, MA**

## Kevin's Van

For the past nine years, a large white block of automotive machinery has presided over our driveway, marking our house to all who pass by. A wide circle—family, friends, neighbors, colleagues, and the crew at our local auto shop—are familiar with this vehicle. No doubt strangers also recognize the van from trying to park beside it in the supermarket lot. They must wonder who drives this hulk on errands around town. The answer is a man who used to be a building contractor until his wife (me) persuaded him to get a job that didn't put him in danger of falling off a roof. Kevin took a nearby position as a school custodian, but that didn't change his mode of transportation. The van remained with us. It had become Kevin, and Kevin had become the van. It was his home away from home. His hideout, his man cave, his travelling tool shed and clothes bin.

Bought used to begin with, the van had served him for over a hundred thousand miles, and its weaknesses had long been identified and accommodated. Kevin shrugged at the drivers in freeway traffic who screamed by in annoyance at the van's slow pace. He ignored the alarming electronic icons that frequently lit up on the dashboard, signaling problems even Roy's Auto Repair couldn't decipher. When the van rusted out in jagged holes, Kevin patched them himself, then painted the lower half on both sides a flat black. It looked like a gigantic saddle shoe.

When I remarked that the old vehicle spent more time at Roy's than at home or school, Kevin was patient but stern. "You don't understand," he said, as if trying to explain gravity to a child. "*Old* is not the problem. I can run the Mercedes engine another hundred thousand miles. Everyone with a Sprinter complains about the electronics, but there's nothing you can do about them."

**Rosemary Sedgwick**
**Boxborough, MA**

However, the deep cold and cumulative snowstorms of this past winter took a toll on the Kevin-van relationship. One undeniable weakness of the vehicle (and the one attribute I found admirable) was that it ran on organic diesel fuel. Kevin had to get up at least once, often twice during the most bone-chilling nights to run the engine. Otherwise, being organic, the fuel froze.

Even worse, the van lacked four-wheel drive. For years, Kevin had pitted his skill at the wheel against all that New England winter could throw at him, and both man and van had survived. Then came the winter of their undoing. After working a late shift until 1:30 a.m., Kevin stepped out into a blizzard which was piling snow on roads that had been half-cleared, turned to ice, and snowed over again.

On his drive home he was alone on the dark backroads; not even a plow was out in the howling, blinding storm. The van bucked and slid, but made it up the steep hill to the road by our house. It got through two feet of new snow all the way to the intersection with the lane that leads to our driveway, and then, just as Kevin was thanking his lucky stars, it jammed in the snowbank at the turn.

He couldn't leave the van there, in the way of snow plows that would arrive when the storm let up. He wriggled out the passenger side door, clomped down the lane and up our driveway.

The automatic garage door opener didn't work. He heaved it up by hand, got out a shovel, cleared a patch in front of the garage large enough for the snowblower. Then, with the wind tearing at him and snow clumping on his eyelids, he set about clearing the driveway and up the lane to where the van loomed ghostly in the night.

"Like using a toothpick to brush a hippo's teeth," he said afterwards.

Kevin waited until spring had come before sharing his decision with me. "I'm going to sell the van and get a truck with four-wheel drive," he said over Sunday breakfast, our

**Rosemary Sedgwick**
**Boxborough, MA**

usual catch-up time for the week. His voice was mournful and apologetic, as if announcing he'd have to shoot his horse.

Things went quickly. He informed Roy, who is the pulsing nerve center for used-vehicle communications in our area, and listed the van on Craigslist. While word seeped out locally, replies to the listing streamed in. If we hadn't experienced globalization before then, we certainly got it via Kevin's van. People sent queries from every continent except Antarctica.

"I guess you didn't include a photo?"

"Don't have to. People who drive Sprinters don't care what they look like. It's the Mercedes engine, I told you."

"Oh. That."

It took him several days, working as hard as Hercules in the Aegean stables, to clear out the van. He was pleased and astonished with the results, reporting occasionally on found treasures. His favorite knife. Boxes of nails worth hundreds of dollars. A t-shirt with "Born to play. Forced to work." on the front.

The next Sunday, a week after the listing, two Ukrainians showed up in our driveway. "Well?" I said, when Kevin returned from driving around with them in the van.

"They say they'll buy it."

"What about the winters?"

"They know Sprinters. They know what they're getting. If they don't end up taking it, someone else will."

The next morning, the Ukrainians came back with envelopes of cash, and signed a bill of sale that quitclaimed Kevin of any problems with the van that might show up later.

Soon afterwards, Kevin heard of a pickup truck being rebuilt by our regional Toyota dealer. It was a good deal, he said, and Roy approved. After getting new tires installed and filling it up with regular gas, Kevin drove the truck home.

It's pretty, a crimson red, sitting in our driveway. But you could easily confuse it with one of the other red pickup trucks in the supermarket parking lot.

**Monica Moeller**
**Lamoine, ME**

## The Shearwater

*First: The Beach House*

The path from your house to the beach
is well-worn, easily-followed, except
it meanders across the field
around the snarl of alders.
I followed it
and felt each change in direction
with a touch of dizziness
as if I were lost.

*Second: The Conversation*

We each turned and looked to the sea
not each other.
A September sun glancing
across the water burned my cheek,
the line of my jaw,
while a cap shaded my eyes
from your anger.

Questions not meant to be answered,
still voiced with uplifted pitch
as if there was an answer
unsaid but understood.

In the distance
the graceful line of a seabird,
a shadow gliding above the surface
against the late sun, solitary.
We know the shearwater
by that silhouette. She almost

(continued)

**Monica Moeller**
**Lamoine, ME**

never comes ashore except to
breed, never
at home on land.

*Third: The Decision*

As you walked away from me
your shadow angled across the hillside
of sun-baked grass. It is
the way you touch the earth,
the way you split the sun,
the way I see you now,
obliquely.

***

**Gordon Clark**
**Damariscotta, ME**

## February Dawn on the Damariscotta

Blind bright the sharp sun's rays
Frozen the solid air
Aged copper the needles of pine, spruce and fir
Chandelier crystal the dormant maple, apple and birch
Window pane glass the river
Carrara marble white the
driveway banks of hard winter snow
Silent the chickadees, creatures of the air
Huddled the squirrels, creatures of the ground
Still upon still upon still
and yet
awakening, gliding, drifting, coiling sea smoke
rolling out low from the back cove
telling of time beyond the moment.

**Karen E. Wagner**
**Hudson, MA**

## White Woods

Wind picks up,
clears the lawn of holiday
decorations two weeks early.
Bits of sun slice through clouds
impose shadows amidst the gloom.
Leaves I've raked push
back to swaddle the grass.
Last of the marigolds
weep for summer.

There'll be snow tonight.
I'd hardly given a thought
to how my woods will change.
They've been my summer shelter,
permitted me the illusion
of writing in a tree house.
Now I watch the turkey
stride below the branches,
into the brush and out of sight.

Snow comes hard.
Moon swallowed
by fronts of shredded inspiration.
Shrouds the ground, builds
a world for me
of white woods
with sticks of bark
against a pearl sky.

**Helen Ackermann**
**Rothschild, WI**

## Patient Waiting

Waiting is not valued in our society. While driving we have probably all had the experience of being followed very closely by someone who is not in favor of waiting for anything. The driver wants to quickly pass and continue at a speed that is not in keeping with the marked miles per hour. Waiting in a grocery line causes consternation and frustration. Waiting for someone at a meeting or for a luncheon date causes further frustration. No, waiting is not valued according to modern thought, and yet can there be value in waiting?

Well-known spiritual writer, Henri Nouwen, tells us this about waiting. "Waiting is essential to the spiritual life." We need to wait with patience. Nouwen tells us that waiting comes from the Latin verb *patior* which means "to suffer." He claims that "waiting patiently always means paying attention to what is happening right before our eyes and seeing there the first rays of God's glorious coming." We need to suffer through the present to reach the future.

Simone Weil, a Jewish writer, said, "Waiting patiently in expectation is the foundation of the spiritual life." And so we learn to wait. We wait until our fears pass, we wait until illness becomes bearable, we wait until a broken relationship mends or is accepted. We wait in anticipation for something to change. As we wait we are challenged to "...stand erect and raise our heads because your redemption is at hand." Luke 21:28 We wait with patience and with trust that God's goodness will be revealed.

**Mark D. Biehl**
**Hales Corners, WI**

## Sandhill

Announced by raucous clarion
They float with uncommon silence
To fields
Just tilled—
Landing with a confidence
Born of generations.

Uncountable numbers
Of pencil-legged clerics
Uniformly dowdy
In dusty brown  robes—
Crimson yarmulkes

Gathering to plan
In groups of solemnity-

Then rising
With that same throaty cry,

And fading away
With grace.

***

**Sylvia Little-Sweat**
**Wingate, NC**

## Artist

An Autumn still-life:
Mother's palette, brushes, paints
Packed in Memory.

**Genie Dailey**
**Jefferson, ME**

## Empty Windows

Sad house,
your windows blinded
from the inside
by unseen hands...
why some with shades
and some with sagging curtains?
Empty now,
your windows see and feel
nothing, no one
inside or out.
Where did your soul go
when your family moved?
Does it still wander within
your echoing rooms,
your rattling hallways,
keening for companionship,
for life and breath,
a human touch?

If human eyes
are windows to the soul,
what happens when our eyes
become as empty windows?

**Andrea Suarez-Hill**
**Jonesboro, ME**

## One Last December Day

Silence roars at dawn
over iced flats
as high tide skates
on crusty mud and
mute gulls mingle with chimney smoke.
Bare hands and fingers burn,
trees snap, cracked boots creak.
Along a tree-lined ridge
firs felled by salt from
new moon overflows
sleep in fall's washouts.
Their root wads reach
like crippled feet.
Sun's grey ghost
slips above a tidal basin.
Stalled fog, frozen dust,
paints opaque equine shapes
in cotton light.
White shadows stir and
nicker for first feed.
A buried voice speaks
its tears behind eyes and throat,
wets my cheeks and
begs this peace bide another year.

**Jane Potter**
**Bar Harbor, ME**

## Frances vs. the Ice

Frances Connor hated being fussed over, yet here she was tucked up in her recliner, legs outstretched on the footrest, bandaged ankle hidden under layers of blankets. Her daughter Susan was responsible for all the coddling, reversing their roles and treating Frances like a child.

Although Frances was eighty years old and widowed, she still occupied her lakeside house and prided herself on being a young eighty, able to live independently. However, the morning's emergency visit to the hospital in Bar Harbor could change things: Frances knew that Susan would use the accident to encourage Frances to move.

"I'm *fine*, you go back to your meeting or whatever you were doing," Frances insisted.

Susan was a busy real estate agent with an office a short drive away in Bar Harbor

"No, you aren't fine!" Susan said. "What were you thinking, going out to the mailbox when you know Eddie will fetch your mail?" Eddie, twenty, was a neighbor; he earned extra money doing odd jobs for Frances.

"Mom," Susan continued, "you may feel fine now, but remember how much your ankle hurt. You don't know how lucky you are that it didn't break!"

Frances heard the words, but she knew Susan was saying something entirely different: Frances shouldn't continue to spend winters in Maine, or if she insisted on staying in Maine, she should move to a sheltered community. But for Frances, nowhere could match the view of her beloved lake; it was an all-season source of enjoyment, and the recliner was positioned so she could see the lake from her large picture window.

They'd had the argument so many times that Frances could recite Susan's lines as well as her own. "I'm not leaving

**Jane Potter**
**Bar Harbor, ME**

the lake and *that's that*!" always ended the discussion. Frances had been able to hang on, but this injury might push Susan over the line.

Susan arose with a sigh and shrugged. "I need to get back to work. I've arranged with the neighbors to bring you some food later. Are you *sure* you can get to the bathroom on your own?"

Frances could barely contain herself. "Go! I'm not an infant!" She grabbed the railing of the walker that Susan had placed within reach and rattled it like the bars of a cage. That eased her frustration for a moment. "Sorry darling. I feel so helpless," she mumbled.

Susan softened her voice and placed her arm around Frances's narrow shoulders. "I know you do Mom, but if you stay off your foot and let your ankle heal like the doctor said, this phase shouldn't last long."

"Humph," Frances said, fighting tears and staring out at the lake. But as she heard Susan open the front door to leave, she turned her head and called out, "Thank you darling, I mean it!" Frances didn't know if Susan heard or not, but at least it had been said.

All Frances had done was walk along the short driveway to her roadside mailbox. Eddie kept the driveway clear of snow, and he was generous with sanding icy areas. Frances would mutter to herself that he was turning her front path into Sand Beach. He obviously hadn't expected Frances to go to the mailbox, where a November cold spell had left a patch of ice.

Frances leaned her head back and closed her eyes. *When had ice become an enemy?*

Seems she never thought about her relationship with ice until now. In Maine it was part of life: you drove carefully over it, and if you walked on it you wore boots that gripped well, or, more recently, you strapped on those new-fangled ice grippers. Susan had bought a pair for her, but she found the bindings too difficult for her arthritic hands.

**Jane Potter**
**Bar Harbor, ME**

At least she could still grasp a mug of hot tea, and she mentally thanked Susan for that act of kindness. A teapot sat within reach in its blue knitted cozy (Susan must have unearthed it from a box of donations for a charity sale Frances was organizing), as well as a small pitcher of cream and a bowl of sugar. Frances sighed. Bundled in blankets, feet up mid-day, *tea cozies* for Heaven's sake. Only old people lived like this.

She looked out at the lake again: open water still, but in a few weeks, or earlier if the temperature stayed cold, it would freeze over. Ice fishing huts would populate the lake and she smiled at the memory of her late husband waiting impatiently to get his own hut onto the ice. He would bide his time by repainting it, repairing broken wood, polishing the door handle and hinges until it was the smartest hut on the ice.

Not that anyone really looked at the huts: what counted were the fish he could catch. She remembered how proud he was to walk into the kitchen, chilled to the bone, and present her with the bounty from the lake. She wondered if primitive man would admire his skills, or would they ask why he was out there fishing in the cold, when he had a pantry full of food?

Yes, ice was a good friend in those days. It gave pleasure in so many ways: her husband's love of ice fishing, the neighbors with their ice skating, the youngsters who would come flying down the opposite hillside on sleds, straight onto the ice and continuing at speed until they crashed into the snowy edge of her yard.

They would leap up laughing and screaming, brush off the snow, and do it all over again, not bothered by sprained ankles *or worse*: Susan's code for a broken leg, a broken spine, or a broken neck. Frances shuddered; maybe she should count herself lucky that it was only a sprained ankle.

"You must have very strong bones!" the young doctor had declared as he bandaged it earlier that morning. He had seemed almost disappointed that the X-ray showed no fracture in someone so elderly, as if Frances was betraying all he'd learned in medical school. *Hah!* She thought to herself, grinning. *Guess I showed him!*

She realized she was hungry; it was getting close to lunchtime, according to the grandfather clock. There was a knock on the door that connected the kitchen to the garage, and then the door opened: probably Eddie's mother bringing food as Susan had arranged.

Eddie's family used the garage entrance because their visits usually coincided with doing yardwork or dropping off items for the charity sale. With her large and now carless garage, Frances had agreed to store donations that people could leave without disturbing her.

"I'm in here, Angela!" Frances called, and turned her head in surprise at the reply.

"It's me, Mrs. C.," came Eddie's cheerful deep voice. He worked as a maintenance worker for the town and wore his brown overalls, so he must be on his own lunch break.

"Are you here to drop off my lunch?" she asked, smiling up at him; he was tall and he towered over her, especially in her reduced and bundled state. "Apparently I'm to be treated as an *invalid*," she added with a laugh.

"Yes, I brought lunch," Eddie said, crouching down to meet her at eye level. "I'm so sorry I missed clearing that ice. Thank God you didn't break anything!"

Frances groaned. "You and Susan, expecting the worst. I'm tough! Anyway," she said, taking his strong rough hand in hers, "it is *not* your fault! The post office should keep the area clear."

"I'm not sure about that, Mrs. C. They deliver the mail from their trucks and I don't think the carrier steps out at your mailbox."

"Maybe you're right, Eddie. I know you're busy, so I don't want to keep you long. Just put whatever your mom made on a plate and bring me a fork. I'll be fine after that."

**Jane Potter**
**Bar Harbor, ME**

Eddie let her hand go and stood up. "Can you wait a few minutes to eat?"

"Sure," Frances said, "or longer if you need to go and do something first."

"Nope, I'll be in the kitchen."

Frances closed her eyes and leaned her head back again. The sun streamed through the window and she dozed off in the warmth; her breathing became shallow.

She woke to tapping on her shoulder. *"Mrs. C., oh no, are you all right?"* Eddie was whispering.

She jolted awake and smiled up at the scared boy. "I'm not dead yet, sonny!"

He laughed with relief, then slid a TV snack table closer and positioned it over her lap. "This is awful," she moaned. "I feel like an ancient biddy in a nursing home."

"You, ancient? Never!" Eddie said, then he went back to the kitchen and returned carrying a tray which he placed on the snack table. The first sensation Frances noticed was fragrance; Eddie had filled a crystal bud vase with yellow freesias.

"Where did you get these?" she cried with delight, lifting the vase to inhale the scent.

"A girl at work received a bouquet, and she said I should take a few to share with you."

"Please thank her for me," Frances said, and turned her attention to the meal. Expecting (dreading) a portion of one of Angela's bland casseroles, she was surprised to see a bowl of hot penne pasta in a cream sauce, with smells of garlic and rosemary that soon eclipsed the freesias. The pasta was sprinkled with grated parmesan and decorated with parsley tucked around the edges.

There was a slice of garlic toast, and a demitasse cup of clear red broth. Eddie pointed to it. "Drink your *amuse-bouche* first. Freshly-made seedless tomato soup."

"I'm speechless!" Frances said. "*You* prepared this, in my kitchen?"

**Jane Potter**
**Bar Harbor, ME**

"Yes Mrs. C.," he replied, blushing, "but you should be eating it instead of talking about it. I'll be back soon to pick up the tray and make you coffee or whatever you want for later."

Frances took her time and savored the food bite by bite. When was the last time she'd had an *amuse-bouche*? Maybe never. And of far more interest, what was Eddie doing making an *amuse-bouche* in the first place? He certainly hadn't learned that from his mother.

She had her answer when Eddie returned half an hour later: he wanted to train as a chef, but he didn't know how to tell his parents; they expected him to work in town close to home.

And he needed to tell them so that he could create dishes for an upcoming cooking competition. "You can use my kitchen," Frances suggested. "I'll pay for the food if you cook meals so I can rest my ankle. Deal?"

"Deal!" he said, and they shook hands.

As the wintry days turned into weeks and the temperature stayed below freezing, the lake gradually solidified; the ice fishermen and women and the skaters ventured on and found it safe. Soon the children were sledding down the hill and onto the ice. Her ankle recovering, Frances was back on her feet but staying indoors under Susan's orders.

Children were using plastic sleds instead of the wooden sleds that Frances remembered from childhood. Against the pure white snow of the hillside, the brightly colored sleds were a cheery and welcome contrast. The plastic sleds seemed to have minds of their own, and Frances watched the children sliding all over the lake, coming to a stop out on the ice, or crashing into the frozen reeds and shrubs at the edges of the lake.

What fun! Now and again the youngsters would notice Frances at the window, and they'd wave; she would wave back. She had an eerie sense of waving across time at her younger self, not just through the glass. A lifetime on the ice

**Jane Potter**
**Bar Harbor, ME**

was displayed in all its stages: sledding as a youngster, skating as an adult, then walking gingerly to visit her husband in his ice hut, bringing a thermos of coffee.

She'd seen a red plastic sled among the charity donations; silly to have it sit for weeks when a child could use it now. The donation boxes were lined up on tables in the garage.

Wedged between two boxes, Frances found the sled with the long rope pull intact. She hauled it out from between the boxes and dragged it through the kitchen and into the front room.

It was two o'clock; on his days off Eddie had been arriving earlier, using as much time as he could get to practice his recipes. Frances expected him soon. She went into her bedroom; after layering on her warmest clothes she emerged ready for an outing, cocooned inside a puffy purple down coat borrowed from a charity box.

On his arrival Eddie burst into laughter. "Mrs. C., you look like you're going to the Antarctic! What's with all the layers?"

"I need a favor." She pointed out the window towards the sledding hill, then at the sled. "I want to take this for the kids to use. Will you drive me up there?"

"Why don't I make you a cup of tea and I'll take the sled up there for you?" Eddie asked.

"Don't you go *cup of tea-ing* me," she said, wagging a gloved finger at him. "You're as bad as Susan. I want the pleasure of seeing a child's face when I hand over the sled."

Eddie sighed and considered her request. Frances was counting on Eddie's reluctance to say no and risk losing use of her kitchen. "All right," he said, "but promise me you'll hold my arm the whole time, okay?"

"Promise!" Frances said. Eddie grabbed the sled and they went out to his truck. He lifted Frances up into the passenger seat and fastened her seatbelt. She didn't protest even though he made her feel like a toddler.

**Jane Potter**
**Bar Harbor, ME**

Eddie drove up the sloping road at the side of the lake and parked the truck at the top. They carefully walked across packed snow to the staging area for the sledding and reached a group of children waiting their turn on the sleds.

Frances stared at the lake. Her nemesis the ice stretched out in front of her, tempting her with its white innocence, daring her to step on it again, challenging her to enter its cold, unforgiving world.

Eddie put the sled down and whispered to Frances, "Who do you want to give the sled to first?"

She looked at the children, their faces eager with anticipation, and she looked at the frozen lake.

Suddenly she yelled, "You don't scare me, ice!" She pulled free of Eddie's arm and dropped herself onto the sled. She stretched her arms up and threw her head back. "Whee! Whee!" she cried as the sled escaped the reach of Eddie's outstretched arms, gaining momentum as it barreled down the hill.

"Mrs. C.! NO!!" But by now Frances was a puffy purple blur on a bright red sled, careening across the ice. She grasped the sides of the sled, rocking it back and forth, changing direction, daring the ice to do its worst. She sped towards an ice hut, bumped into it, and ricocheted off in another direction. Eventually, the sled slowed with the friction on the ice and ground to a halt mid-lake.

A group of skaters hurried across the ice to rescue her. Frances recognized them from the neighborhood. A young man grabbed the rope pull from where it lay in the front of the sled, then he turned in the direction of Frances's yard. Frances leaned forward and tugged on the rope to get his attention.

"Alan, I'm not ready to go home!" she cried. "Let go!"

"But Frances, you're stuck out here! It's cold and you'll fall if you try walking home on the ice."

Another skater said something to Alan, and he spoke to Frances again. "Would you like me to pull you for a little

**Jane Potter**
**Bar Harbor, ME**

while?"

"Oh yes please!" she said.

"Okay, hold on tight!"

Frances settled herself back into the sled. Alan headed for the edge of the lake and began a slow gliding pace around the perimeter, towing the sled as Frances yelped with glee. What a treat to see parts of the lakeside she hadn't visited for years. Other skaters joined in the fun; Frances glanced back to see several skaters holding hands and following her sled in an undulating line.

For so long she'd experienced the skaters visually from her living room. She'd forgotten about the sounds and sensations of skating: the rhythmic metallic click and swoosh when the blades engaged the ice, left, right, left, right, and the spray of ice flakes in the wake, falling on Frances like confetti. She felt like the star in a parade.

People emerged from ice huts to stare; Frances recognized a couple of her husband's old buddies and she waved. "Look at me, I'm on the ice!" she called, laughing.

The skating parade continued around the edge of the lake, and soon Frances saw Susan and Eddie watching from the edge of her yard. Judging from Susan's best gray suit and all the jewelry she wore, Frances knew she'd been pulled out of a meeting or an open house. Again.

"Uh-oh," Frances muttered as they reached her yard. "Fun's over." She steeled herself for Susan's tirade.

Alan brought the sled to a gentle stop. Frances looked up at Susan and was surprised to see her wiping away tears: tears of joy, fury, or fear? She couldn't tell.

Eddie leaned over the sled and scooped her into his arms. "Mrs. C., you gave us all a fright!" The skaters watched to make sure Frances was safe.

Susan smiled through her tears and grasped Frances's hand tightly. "Come on, Mom," she said. "You've had an adventure! I'll make you a nice cup of tea."

**Michael H. Mitias**
**Jackson, TN**

## I am a Marionette

When love in your heart kindles,
Its fire rages wildly,
Triumphantly,
Ideas in your mind fumble,
Emotions in your heart shrivel,
And desires in your will wrinkle.

Then you become a flame,
A burning flame,
The flame you are,
The flame you should be—
Alone, naked, pure—
A shining flame
Of light,
Passion,
Truth.

Then, space shrinks to naught,
Time halts to a standstill,
And earth under your feet crumbles!
Alas! Heaven becomes earth
And earth heaven!

And then before the divine altar
You kneel,
You pray,
In praying you understand,
And then your heart declares:

**Michael H. Mitias**
**Jackson, TN**

I am a marionette that cannot
Move without Your touch,
Feel without Your warmth,
Think without Your vision,
Will without Your compassion,
Sing without Your wine,
And live without Your care!

***

**John Gillespie**
**Camden, ME**

## graveyard

a colloquial sky squats on the horizon

the trees silhouette and huddle by the steeple

a tubercular wind banters among the tombstones
as they slump and await yet another winter.

so many stories that end the same way:
cold, vacant, and alone.

their histories jump on you as you pass
and you carry them with you for a few steps

before their shadows slip away
somewhere between Smith & McElreavy
and disappear into the gaping earth.

**P. C. Moorehead**
**North Lake, WI**

## Come

Come walking with white breath.
White Breath,
come walking.

Older soldier, come.
Come walking.

Younger soldier, come too.
Come walking.

Lift up your hands.
Lay down your arms.

Walk—unarmed—closer.
Breathe.

White Breath,
breathe,

unarmed,
closer,
come.

**Bobby A. Troutt**
**Gallatin, TN**

## Bud

Winter has passed and spring has come. And, I am but a small young bud on a twig of a tall tree, like so many others, waiting to open to my new life. As the warmth of the spring breeze slowly moves me, the light from the sun begins to slowly open me up and I grow and grow until I fully open. During my days of spring, I dress the tree with all of my fullness. And in summer, too, I dangle from a limb in the hot summer days. Slowly, I move about as a slight breeze blows by. But, it would be in autumn when my true beauty is revealed. In autumn, as I dangle from a twig, I slowly move with the breeze as the sun enhances my brilliant colors for all to see. Now, I am a burnt orange with a little touch of crimson and my friends around me are yellow, light green, crimson red and bright orange. Yes, it is in autumn that my beauty so beholds to bring joy to all who look upon me. When autumn shall pass, winter grows near and the time comes for my fall, my stem will break away from the twig and I will slowly float to the ground and lie there with the rest of my friends. In my fall, I will slowly float down and I may, too, spin about. And, when I hit the ground, I may stay there for a while until a cool breeze comes by and flips me over and over. I will ballet across the ground for I am nothing but a leaf which has fallen from a tree.

**Linda Shepard**
**Union, ME**

## Maine, Mid-October

The intensity of this day
presses on my chest.
The deep stillness, a perfect calm,
the brilliance of the
crystalline blue sky,
cloudless.
How is it that
beauty creates this ache,
a stirring
a deep longing to remember
something I've lost?

A flock of starlings
disbands from a treetop.
Randomly
they drop in silence
down to the big oak
instantly disappearing.
Their movements let loose
the last of the acorns
they click, tick
as they fall through the branches.

Eight geese glide down
and land by the farm pond.
The cows glance at me
with mild interest,
placidly they pull the grass
their jaws working sideways.
I hear their huffing breath.
A sheep bleats somewhere.

**Linda Shepard**
**Union, ME**

My eyes move
to the sunlit red sumac
sticks of flame
which brighten the woods.
The last purple asters,
bees still busy in them,
bow to the ground
with flower laden stems.

The trees are on fire again.
How is it
that we are not riveted,
open-jawed and awed
eyes amazed
by this colorful blaze?

How is it
that the once green leaves,
the earth's lung and breath
transmute their lives
into this silent, beautiful death
releasing the trees to open sky?

***

**Sylvia Little-Sweat**
**Wingate, NC**

## Pawley's Island

In evanescent
Spring even the egret's cry
Is hushed by the Marsh.

**Anne Mullin**
**Bonita Springs, FL**

## Before the Plow

The snow-covered road
has lost all linearity to become
white space between trees
drawing the eye up and above
vanished ground into swirls
of flakes aimless in dull gray
light suspending the viewer
in vertigo.

The hilly street I lived on
once went unplowed for days
after a blizzard shut down the city.
Freed from school we sledded without limit
until we tired of snow caked on our mittens,
down our collars and boots, grew bored
with boundlessness, disenchanted
with cold, with white.

But today looking up
through formless spatters of snow
falling into oblivion I know
the town crew will come soon
to reestablish edges and
direction. Reason to cherish
these rare moments of giddiness
before the plow.

**J. Adams**
**Edgecomb, ME**

## The Last Hike, the First Sign

I died a little on July 7, 2013. My wife and I were on our annual anniversary hike when it all happened and the beginning of the end started. It was a beautiful day. As I recall, we knew it would be hot but that was to be expected in early July. We got up early and drove to Rangeley, Maine and started our planned hike, heading northbound from a parking lot on Route 4, at a road crossing of the Appalachian Trail (AT). Our destination was Piazza Rock for a picnic lunch, then on to the summit of Saddleback Mountain, often referred to by seasoned hikers as, "The flattest mile on the AT."

The day started okay, with some fog that would soon burn off, leaving us with a very humid day. As I hiked, I noted that the evergreen forest felt more like an Amazon jungle; very steamy. Sweat poured off my head like an early June thunderstorm, without the hail. Early in the hike, I began noticing an odd trend. I had trouble keeping up with my wife. This was highly irregular. I could usually out hike her walking backwards with twice the weight! Whenever we'd overnighted together, I would carry all the heavy stuff, which we'd found to be a strategy that equalized our speed quite well. But today we were packed evenly and wearing only daypacks, so my lack of ability to keep up was odd. We made Piazza Rock and decided to stop for lunch, which resulted in a fairly long break, taking time to explore our surroundings. After fueling our bodies, we continued on toward Saddleback Mountain, but by now my body was saying, "Bad Idea!" I made a mental check list of myself as I usually did when things weren't going quite right. No sign of a head cold. I noted that my bum left knee was bothering earlier than it usually did when I hiked, but not enough to cause alarm. I simply couldn't pinpoint my crappy feeling and noted that its intensity was growing increasingly stronger as the day progressed.

Gracie was stopping regularly to snap pictures while I caught up. At one point, she took a picture of a cute frog on a steep side hill. The frog leaped, landed unsteadily, then tumbled head over tea kettle; poor thing! Moments later, Gracie dropped her camera and dented a corner near the view screen proving fatal to the camera years later.

As we arrived near a pond on the trail, I noticed my symptoms were continuing to grow stronger with an obvious increasing of intensity. I told her I needed a break and had to put something in my stomach, hoping it would help. I took out a map and located the pond. We had been hiking steadily for several hours and although my body was exhausted, the map showed very little distance had been covered. I ate some food and felt better...until I started hiking again. I practically fell down and said, "I can't go any farther... I feel awful...I will be lucky to make it back to the car." I sat down, cooled off and calmed myself. The last time I had pulled the plug on a hike, I had eaten some bad sausage and my brother had practically carried me off Katahdin. While I rested, Gracie explored a bit further up the trail and came back worried and inquisitive about what was going on. I told her I was unsure but I knew I was having a bad one. "You can continue," I told her, "but I have to go back; I might not even get back today. By the way I feel, I may have to spend the night out here." She knew I was bad off and the matter was quite serious.

Ninety percent of injuries occur on the way down. I knew this and did not want to add to my steadily increasing agony. Usually heading back gave a sense of relief, a morale boost when you know that every step is getting you closer to the car. By late afternoon, my condition had worsened and I was stumbling and staggering all over the trail. Vertigo created a world that was blurred. I was dizzy and the terrain very uneven. My eyes hurt, my legs would not work, and I could hardly feel my left side. With every step, it only got worse. I felt like what a person looked like when they had a stroke. For the first time, I let Gracie take most of the stuff from my pack, I could not think and could not make decisions, so she took control of the situation and simply did what needed to be done. Eventually, she had to take my entire pack as my body seemed to be slowly shutting down, refusing to function normally.

Hours passed with just a mile or two covered. The sun was getting low in the sky and the mountain coolness seemed to reach out, lift me up and brush me off. I was getting better as the coolness of evening was setting in! Incredibly, I was soon back to a functioning human being again. Gracie insisted on carrying my pack, while offering encouragement, letting me know that we were making good time now and would soon be back to the car. At that point, I was feeling much better, just very tired so I opted to drive as we journeyed toward home.

I noted that my eyes were jumpy but with the window rolled down and the cool, evening breeze caressing me as I drove, my functioning slowly increased. We were just outside Augusta when I had to turn the car lights on. Suddenly, I started feeling as I'd felt on the mountain and warned Gracie that I was not doing well and that she would have to drive. The oncoming car headlights were incredibly bothersome.

Since we were celebrating our anniversary, we decided to stay at a hotel. We were both tired and although it would've been only another hour to our doorstep, we decided the hotel room was a good option. What a wise move it was! I lay on the nice hotel bed with my eyes closed, my left side felt tingly, combined with a sort of crawling sensation. I continued to wonder what was going on with my body but from that moment on, I knew something strange was going on.

I have had a few substantial hikes since that fateful July day, but never the same as before it. My wife and I did a gorgeous hike, actually one of my favorites, ten plus miles on fairly flat terrain. I climbed Katahdin with my daughter on

**J. Adams**
**Edgecomb, ME**

June 21, 2014 and that hike was close to disaster. I got off the mountain under my own power but she drove back to a hotel in Millinocket and assisted me back to a functioning state. A year later, I climbed Katahdin with my son. I had purposely waited until September for cooler weather but unfortunately it was an extremely hot September day even on the summit, which is rare. When we reached the parking lot, my unlicensed son drove me to the local hospital where my brother drove my wife nearly four hours to meet us and with lots of medical assistance, I survived.

Since July 7, 2013, a part of me has died. Before that date, I was a strong, avid hiker, but that ability has been stolen from me as time has progressed, seemingly beginning on that day. In the fall 2013, I saw my doctor about this issue. His suggested diagnosis was confirmed in the fall of 2015. It took two years of intensive testing and I was on a first name basis with the folks that ran the MRI machine. I saw seven different specialists who all confirmed the diagnosis of Multiple Sclerosis.

Now, I gratefully explore the Camden Hill's on the coast of Maine but yearn for the higher peaks of summits like Katahdin. Hiking has taken on a whole new realization for me now. Gone are the 16-mile day hikes and 15-minute miles are a thing of the past. Eighty-year-olds pass me like I am tied to a tree but if I am slow and careful and go out on a cool enough day, I can feel the mountain breezes blow through my hair again and get to a high enough elevation where I can have the privilege of looking down on God's great creation.

**Steve Troyanovich**
**Florence, NJ**

## how does tomorrow dream?
*for John Trudell*

*The price the heart pays*
*How does tomorrow dream*
**—John Trudell**

already cold
remorseless moonbeams
huddle against foothills
framing vistages
of mythical slumber...

ashes of moonlight
embracing embers
time dreams
in sedative shadows—
the night sky ambushed
by dawn's thulean touch...

intertwining sorrows
mingle stars with tears
the moon scalds
in sleepless coldness...

shadowlight and
perfumed memories
empty into human form—
pain fills a gaping hole
pouring what is lost
into the angel's final kiss...

***how does tomorrow dream?***

**Meg Weston**
**Camden, ME**

## Moon Shot

The summer men landed on the moon
I launched from my family in Connecticut,
drove 2,452 miles with my friend Candy
in her car named Mortimer, and landed
at Reed College in Portland, Oregon
under a cloud of drizzling August rain.
Letters from home were already waiting
for me, and more arrived daily with men
on the moon stamps, planting our flag
238,900 miles away from earth. Perhaps
I needed to be that far away to keep myself
from getting pulled back in by the gravity
of my mother's letters: Air Mail, Fair Mail,
Share Mail, Bare Mail, Scare Mail, Beware
mail. Always signed "the White Queen"
after the character in Alice's wonderland,
who, befuddled, would believe each day
six impossible things before breakfast.
Like my mother: the impossible demons
she fought, with a pot of coffee, two packs
of cigarettes, daily doses of Valium. On torn
steno paper, red pen, red ink, she scrawled
her heart out, wrote about my sister trying
to fit into skirts I left behind, of my brother
visiting Dear Dr. Dulit twice a week, to treat
depression, and dodge the draft. Of battles
with my father, desperate to find herself.
She told me Daddy didn't think she should
have let me go so far away But sometimes,
she wrote, you have to cut the cord, again,
and again, and again. She told me to save

(continued)

**Meg Weston**
**Camden, ME**

her letters—each one got darker, my tears
welled up black ink, blurred words, I didn't
understand until I read them years later:
nothing a 17-year-old girl could do but
fly to the moon or head back home again.

***

**Sister Irene Zimmerman**
**Greenfield, WI**

## Awakening

Annie has started school and I, at four,
am free to explore the farmyard, barn
and sheds alone. A skinny cat pads intently
toward the old tool shed. I follow her inside.

She climbs a rusty plow and jumps down
onto a broken car seat where high-pitched
mewing greets her. Squirming kittens tumble
over and under one another, stepping

heedlessly on ears and still unopened eyes.
The mewing stops as tiny paws begin to knead
and mouths to drink in sync. The cat purrs
contentedly in rhythm to my petting.

Above me, in the semi-darkness, pigeons
intermittently coo and flutter their wings.
Light filters through a dusty window.
My young soul milks the cool serenity.

**Robert Hinson**
**Monroe, NC**

## In Remembrance of the War

In remembrance of a soldier who
Through the blood, sweat and pain
Fought a great war for you and me
Though many say in vain.

This man, a young warrior, was
Quite sane before the war,
But as many a brave vet does,
Went crazy from the gore.

Through the jungles of Vietnam
Marched men and boys alike
'Cross fields and streams they all had come
To take another's fight.

After years of cold, hard war
And months of painful fear,
The soldiers came home mentally mangled
To a land once held so dear.

Once in Washington, D. C. where
Our grunt became a cop,
He took a trip to a place there—
A Vietnam veterans' memorial plot.

The dark monument bore a list
Of men killed in the war.
It's not accurate, thought he
For there should have been one more.

**Robert Hinson**
**Monroe, NC**

With his service gun at his side
His head filled with 'Nam's roar,
The grunt committed suicide
In remembrance of the war.

***

**Steve Troyanovich**
**Florence, NJ**

## the last snowstorm

against transparent skies
tearful winds
scatter the final snowflakes
unfurled from the heart...

winter overtakes us
chilled and numb
sad whispers fade
pallid through gaunted trees...

hold my hand
the torment is almost gone
down that road
children play
in a soft meadow
of glistening warmth...
now your body... so tired...
can rest...

**Karen E. Wagner**
**Hudson, MA**

## Hummingbird

Tiny wings of iridescent colors,
flurry of beak and feathers,

hover over half-opened blossoms,
suck life-giving sap,

dart from one to another
in search of the sweetest.

She swishes up to my head
stops inches from my nose.

In the snap of a moment,
I'm judged inedible.

Awed at the boldness
of so minute a creature.

She retreats, floats,
then dashes to the next flower.

I watch her work the garden.
She's dismissed me

for the dozens of untried blossoms
that offer up their nectar.

**Jim Harnedy**
**Machiasport, ME**

## The Scent of Winter

*Transition Time*

Columbus Day weekend officially marks the transition of seasons. The summer folks pack up and close down their camps and cottages and head to their permanent homes. The leaf peepers quickly bid their farewell to the last joy of Maine's autumn fun. It's now the time when frugal and practical Mainers start their seasonal changes—clearing out the garden, swapping the storm door for the screen, putting the snow shovel in a handy spot, and getting the snow blower and sled tuned up for what's to come.

When early November arrives and freezing nights set in, we crank up the woodstoves. Taking a walk on a crisp morning here in Bucks Harbor, one is provided with the smell of seasoned wood burning, the fragrance of freshly tipped balsam branches, integrated with our salt air. This is the annual welcome to the scent of winter.

Daily one can observe pickup trucks rolling by Port Road, here in Bucks Harbor, laden down with balsam tips. Here in Down East, Maine these tips will be creatively made into Christmas wreaths and holiday products. By mid-November these creative products, and Christmas trees are loaded onto 18 wheelers for shipment to retail customers across the country. This is a major product that is an economic factor that provides employment for a number of folks Down East before the long winter sets in.

The Thanksgiving weekend officially welcomes the start of Maine's other fun season. Many of our downhill slopes for skiing and snowboarding open to welcome locals and folks from away to another fun-packed season. The weekend also sees lots of folks out holiday shopping and picking out their Christmas tree. Many locals, as well as families from southern New England, have made it a tradition to come and pick

**Jim Harnedy**
**Machiasport, ME**

out their tree at a local tree farm. Small towns across the state host numerous fun and cultural events, including tree lighting and Santa Claus arrivals that make the holidays in Maine special.

By mid-December Mother Nature has usually graced all of Maine with a blanket of snow which encourages snowmobilers to launch their winter activities. Our well-maintained miles of trails combined with modern sleds now allow sledding with only a 6-8-inch base of snow. Maine's miles of hardened multi-use trails provide sledders, cross-country skiers, snowshoers and hikers with a great opportunity to get out and have fun activities even before the official calendar date of winter.

On bright sunny days before Christmas, my late wife, Jane, and I loved to get out and have a short hike with our dogs at either Roque Bluffs or at Starboard. Unfortunately, I am no longer up to hiking, but I can still appreciate this time of the year watching the seasonal changes from my spectacular view of Bucks Harbor from my living room.

***

**Thomas Peter Bennett**
**Silver Spring, MD**

## Eye Drops

Look up—high, high...
        higher—
up at the ceiling
        Shudder and blink!
Wait three minutes
        eyes squeezed closed.

**Mark D. Biehl**
**Hales Corners, WI**

## Bon Appetite

Black legs sprouting
From lustrous
Auburn coat
In knee deep snow
Stopping—
Suddenly—
Ears searching—

Pouncing-

Dejeuner de lapin

***

**Bob Whitmire**
**Round Pond, ME**

## Tick-Tock

Thirteen years old,
I lie on my aunt's sofa
in her country house,
listening in the dark.
Her antique mantle clock
alternates ticks and tocks—
I won't sleep;
if the clock stops,
so will I.

**F. Anthony D'Alessandro**
**Celebration, FL**

## Is That All There Is?

I drove by my favorite ball fields of yesteryear, teeming with strange faces,
wisps of barbeque smoke spiraled, competing music squawked,
and my memories stood at attention in my mind.
Colors, a kaleidoscope of them, popped out all 'round.
A small army of beach type umbrellas stabbed the soil at various angles.
Pool chairs, far from water, slouched over sun-baked soil.
A panorama of alien faces appeared, I suppose a changing of the guard of sorts.
My tribe fled. I felt jilted, a different herd of yelping kids occupied the tired turf.
The determined pages of the rude calendar left me with an empty-gut feeling.
My guys patrolled these swarming fields during their glory days embracing mountains of awards.
My spindly girl no longer spanks a softball that scatters confused opponents.
My ambidextrous, fleet-footed girl, a mini Mia, no longer kicks dust in the huffing faces of gasping, trailing opponents.
My wee ballplayer no longer forces the big boys to whiff at his fuming fastball.
My blazing grand boy, an Ozark Ike clone, no longer converts singles into homers.
The craggy, paint shedding soccer goal seems to return to its reserved and careworn spot.
Flaking flag football cones staggered sideways like Pisa's Tower.
The baseball field without a whisper of grass, sits encircled by a chipped and chained fence.

**F. Anthony D'Alessandro**
**Celebration, FL**

It still sprawls out like a mini Mississippi prairie.
The fuzzy-faced competitors I'd watched abandoned these grounds seasons ago.
No longer do they blast moon shot stitched baseballs over this disheveled fence.
My group of elders, who'd occupied orange plated chairs, have faded into mental scrapbooks.
Scattered ghosts of grandparents past relocated to reserved celestial seating behind St. Peter's bleachers. I wonder, *Is that all there is?*
The battered baseball backstop, once looking like the tooth less five year-olds that scampered in front of it, underwent a remake, losing some of its seasoned look.
Now, it stands proud, painted, and permanently grandparent free.
Eureka! I spot a new parade of fans lumbering in and stretching out like worker ants on this patchwork of reincarnated playing fields.
Replacement players, like their predecessors, stand knee high to parents and parents of parents as they commandeer the site.
They hunt for an array of rouge baseballs, softballs, and soccer balls.
Another generation of footballers zigzag and stagger across makeshift chalky yard markers, while distorted mouths screech like out of tune choruses.
Life tossed a wicked curve ball my way without a rewind on the horizon.
Time cruelly barged into my days and snatched those moments from me.
Nowadays, my grandchildren perform on expansive and groomed pastures, basking below brilliant neon venues, airline miles away.
I stare at these new troops living their fantasy as I once did.
The words of fabled baseball broadcaster Red Barber ring

**F. Anthony D'Alessandro**
**Celebration, FL**

true, "I've lost my catbird seat." No longer do I
belong here. I guess that's all there is.

***

**Sally Belenardo**
**Branford, CT**

## Born with Fur

Lynxes, foxes,
born with fur beautifully marked
die slowly, in agony, frantic,
legs crushed by steel teeth.

Beavers, seal pups,
born with fur lustrous and smooth
drown in underwater traps
or are bludgeoned as they rise for air.

Minks and rabbits,
born with fur ineffably soft
live in little cages, till gassed and skinned
for those who wear

fur coats as their own.

**Joseph A. Sharron**
**Cape Porpoise, ME**

## Fitzy's Fantasies

One summer we invited sailing friends of ours to join us for a 4th of July dock party on the Kennebunk River in Maine. We had just purchased our dock on the river and were anxious to see our old sailing friends from Cape Anne Marina in Gloucester, MA. After we had made space on our docks, Billy Riley was the first to arrive on his sloop "Miss Conduct." Hockey ran in the veins of Billy's family. His Uncle Jack coached hockey at West Point for almost three decades. Jack also led the U.S. Olympic team to a gold medal by defeating the heavily favored Russians in 1960. Billy also had great success as a coach for the UMass Lowell River Hawks hockey team. He won a NCAA National Championship plus several Divisional titles during his tenure as coach.

Also arriving at our dock following Billy was Bill Sanford and crew aboard the sailing yacht "Cassiopia." Among Billy Riley's crew on the "Miss Conduct" was his long-time friend and assistant hockey coach at West Point, Tom "Fitzy" Fitzgerald. It was the first and only time that Fitzy came to Kennebunkport. At the time, the only thing he knew of the town was that President George H. W. Bush had a summer home there. Now, seeing Fitzy, it was hard to imagine that he was involved with hockey. He looked more like a linebacker coach in the NFL than one who would don a pair of ice skates. He was about six feet four inches tall, heavy shouldered, and walked with an awkward gait. Fitzy was also a very colorful individual known to all his friends as an addictive jokester. I always had difficulty having serious conversations with him as he always had a humorous line following the subject we talked about. Garrison Keeler once said that God created March so that non-drinkers would know what a hangover felt like. I also believe that He sent us Fitzy to give drinkers and non-drinkers a hangover from all the corny

**Joseph A. Sharron**
**Cape Porpoise, ME**

jokes he told.

Being the host of the dock party, I had everyone gather on my sloop, the “Rose of Sharron,” for a day of merriment. Fitzy had everyone laughing before we finished our first Bloody Mary cocktail. By the time he finished his second drink, we started hearing the same old jokes over again. Laughter was contagious and we all still engaged in it for fear of being considered a party poop. By 2:00 am we started to call it a night after hearing Fitzy’s jokes for the third time. The next morning we were all walking the docks like zombies with hangovers that resulted more from the jokes than the cocktails. Fitzy was the exception, for I believe that he became immune to all of his own corny jokes he must have told thousands of times in his lifetime.

First thing in the morning, Fitzy went into Dock Square by himself to do some shopping. He came back with a stack of postcards to mail to his buddies in New Jersey and hockey fans at West Point. He went down below in the galley of my boat to address them. As I looked on, he made no bones about what he was writing to his friends, such as “I had tea with Barbara this morning,” or “I played a round of golf with George this afternoon.” Fitzy was writing away, fantasizing his wonderful visit to Kennebunkport with President Bush. I left him in his glory, knowing that his friends wouldn’t believe a word he was sending them, and he knew it, too. As I was leaving to go up on deck, I mentioned that the president came up the river in his boat frequently. Fitzy just looked at me with a jaundiced eye and went back to his postcards.

A short time later I spotted President Bush’s boat, *Fidelity II*, coming up the river toward our dock followed by several black Zodiac Secret Service boats. I shouted down to Fitzy that the president was coming up the river, and by all the sudden commotion on the docks, Fitzy believed me. He bolted up the companion way on my boat and almost knocked me into the river in the process of having a front row

**Joseph A. Sharron**
**Cape Porpoise, ME**

view. My wife, Xandra, waved the president over and sure enough he came along side and tied up to our boat. President Bush had one passenger with him that we were unable to recognize. In his gentlemanly manner, President Bush introduced everyone on my boat to President Harvel of the new Czech Republic. What a thrill it was for all of us to meet two world leaders unexpectedly. Fitzy was in 7th heaven as he now got "authentic" autographs to boast to his friends. I had a nice poster aboard my boat of President Bush's visit to Raytheon Company where I worked. He signed it and it now hangs framed in my office.

After a nice conversation with both presidents, Fitzy invited them to go out for a sail on my boat in the afternoon. President Bush replied in his best, humble sense of humor, "I don't think so; you all look like a motley crew to me." President Bush said this jokingly, but we all were quite a motley crew after listening to all of Fitzy's jokes the night before.

***

**Bob Whitmire**
**Round Pond, ME**

## Shifting

*After Charles Simic*

Every morning in late winter
sunlight pools
beneath the bottom hinge
of the pantry door;
a black cat soaks up the light,
unless the black dog gets there first.

**Hans Krichels**
**Bucksport, ME**

## Once On Gainesborough Street in Boston

There were so many Leo's back then;
They all seemed to play the harmonica
Or the fiddle.
This particular Leo was from over around Newport,
Neighbor to some friends who had come to visit that wintry day
Down on Gainesborough Street in Boston.
They'd brought Leo with them
To this first floor railroad flat it was
With windows just about head-height
Above the sidewalk outside.
And old Leo sat there with us,
This small wiry man with
Bright eyes sparkling in
His lined and leathery face,
Red and black shirt with suspenders over his shoulders,
Chewing his wad of tobacco and
Taking it all in as we sipped our coffee
And talked about life
In the backwoods of Maine,
None of us noticing Leo's bright eyes
Darting about, looking for.... What?
At the end of his rope at last,
Leo marched to the window,
Threw up the sash,
And shot a dark stream of tobacco juice
Right at the feet
Of a small group of students
From the Berkley School of Music
Just up the street.
Half a dozen of them,

(continued)

**Hans Krichels**
**Bucksport, ME**

Looking up shocked
At this wild-eyed and red-clad gremlin,
Grinning at them from the window above.
If their music in the future
Had occasional discordant notes,
Dervishes dancing through the score.
That would be a tribute to Leo
His shot across their bow, as it was,
Though he would play it differently
On his harmonica
Back home in the boondocks.

***

**Sandy Conlon**
**Steamboat Springs, CO**

## Elijah in the Cave

No earthquake, thunder,
  lightening, or whirlwind,
    no boulders crushed, tumbling from nowhere,
      no wildfires consuming trees and brush.

The God hides himself in shadow and in light
  and quietly in stealth
    moves in and out of days,

A specter like the wind stirring
  the tender pages* of the soul—
    luminous yet stark, alone and still,
      silent and waiting.

*See early use referring to an **attendant**, especially one employed to deliver messages.

**Sylvia Little-Sweat**
**Wingate, NC**

## Phoenix II

Fires blazed behind heart-pine
walls, studs, sills, joists, rafters
charring the mantel and hearth.

The silhouetted dark showed
faces of family and friends as
beds, bureaus, chairs burned.

She barred her heart against
the crackle and pop of sparks
that lit the stark dark sky.

Like an armful of old winter
coats, she held her silent
despair as timbers crashed.

Daybreak, she began to rake
ashes in drifts like snow for
shards of home, of heart.

Alone, she shucked dried
corn for hominy.  A crow
hunched in bitter cold, she

stoked the wash-pot coals.
As lye burned her eyes, smoke
feathered her arms, hands.

**Kathryn Olmstead**
**Caribou, ME**

## County Kindness

It wasn't a big hole, but it was deep and too close to avoid after I saw it—a black space in the white line beside the road. The right front tire took the round hole squarely with a thud, and the warning light on the dash glowed immediately.

My decision to take Route 11 south from Fort Kent was spontaneous. It was only 1:30 p.m. and I had finished delivering the new edition of my magazine, *Echoes*, to stores from New Sweden to Madawaska, Fort Kent and St. Francis. If I made a loop south on Route 11 before returning to Caribou on Route 1, I might be able to reach stores in Patten, Sherman, Island Falls, Oakfield, Houlton and Mars Hill before dark.

Perhaps I'd even see a moose. After seeing two of the gigantic animals stretched out on the beds of trailers, it would be nice to see one still on its feet.

I had just passed the sign for Hedgehog Mountain when the roar that says, "you are about to roll onto your wheel rim" told me to pull off. The rim and center of the wheel were intact, but the tire lay underneath like a wet dishcloth.

Okay. I should be able to do this, I told myself. My friend Francine wouldn't think of calling for help, and she's a tiny little thing.

I dig out the owner's manual and turn to the section titled "Steps to take in an emergency: If you have a flat tire." I move three cartons of magazines from the rear compartment to the back seat and locate the jack, crank, tools and spare tire.

I lean the compact "donut" tire with the distinctive yellow paint job against the front bumper, in clear view of anyone traveling north on Route 11—a visual hint that I could use a hand.

"Chock the tires," says the manual. I look for rocks, but

settle for hunks of sod, probably dug up by the snowplow, and cram them under the left rear tire.

"Slightly loosen the wheel nuts (one turn)." Right. I try one, then another. They won't budge. I fiddle with the jack while deciding I will probably have to call AAA.

"Where are you?" asks the AAA lady, after confirming I am not injured and am safely off the roadway. Grateful to hear a voice since no bars appeared on my cellphone, I tell her I am just south of Winterville Plantation, near Hedgehog Mountain. Asked for specifics, I add north of Patten, south of Eagle Lake.

She calls back in a few minutes: "Are you in Masardis? My supervisor says you gave your location with a range of 75 miles." So I did. I was so focused on Patten, I forgot to mention the towns in between.

"No," I assure her. "I am way north of Masardis. North of Ashland. North of Portage Lake."

"Then can I say you are in Winterville?"

I say yes, even though I had passed the "Au Revoir" sign, a few miles back. "The closest town is Winterville."

In a few minutes I receive a call from a service station in Fort Kent. Help is on the way. I work on the lug nuts a couple more times, then decide to leave the work to someone else and just wait in the car, reading the owner's manual.

Knowing Aroostook County, I was not surprised when a pickup passed me going north, stopped and turned around at the first opportunity.

"Not sure I can do much, but I could not just pass without stopping to see if you were okay," says a jovial man from Allagash. I assure him I'm all set, and we chat as I name a few people I have known with his last name. "Yep, we're related," he affirms. I give him the new edition of *Echoes* as a thank you for stopping and he is on his way.

When a full-length empty logging truck heading north stops and starts to back up, I think, "Oh, no, what if a car comes whipping over the hill?" Not to worry. He angles the double-bed trailer neatly across the road and onto the southbound shoulder perfectly aligned with the rear of my car.

I run up to the cab and thank him profusely for all the trouble he took to reach me, declaring, "I'm all set. Someone is coming from Fort Kent."

"Just to change a tire?" He shakes his head, smiling. "I could have done that."

By now, I am truly sorry I had called for help.

The logger has just disappeared when a young man in a sedan slows down in the northbound lane. "Do you need some help here?" he calls out.

"All set," I respond with thanks. "I have talked to a service station in Fort Kent."

AAA calls to see if the driver has arrived. I look at the time on my cellphone. "How could it be 3:30?" I wonder, until I realize the phone is suddenly picking up a signal from Canada. Still, the predicted wait time has elapsed, and I have dismissed three potential helpers.

Then two cars arrive from opposite directions. A pickup going north turns around and pulls up behind me. A sedan traveling south pulls off the road ahead of my car. The two drivers don't even listen to my story about someone coming from Fort Kent. One handles the jack while the other loosens the wheel nuts.

"Are you together?" I ask.

"Nope," one says. "I'm on my way to work, but can take care of this right quick." Within minutes, the tire is changed and the damaged one stowed in the back of my car along with the tools. Neither man will accept cash, as they sprint to their vehicles. I run after one then the other offering each a magazine as a thank you.

Now what if the driver ordered by AAA arrives and I'm not to be found? I call the service station and am told he should be there any minute. I wait.

Then AAA calls and offers to notify the station to disregard the call for service. I would like to thank the driver for

**Kathryn Olmstead**
**Caribou, ME**

coming, but decide to let AAA cancel the request. Still, I wait a few minutes, hoping to explain that no sooner had I called for help than five people stopped to offer assistance, all within a half hour. If I had only known.

Well, I should have.

***

**Robert B. Moreland**
**Pleasant Prairie, WI**

## League of Her Own

Every day is Opening Day, all new
like the smell of your left-handed glove.
Softball brings the nine-year-old gleam anew,
passion gone wild, second chances for love.

Line up complete, you step up to the plate
stare down the poor pitcher, give him a wink.
There you bite your tongue as you concentrate,
wind up comes flying, white-stitched clincher sinks.

Connect with a crack of an ash-boned bat
with the gusto of a Ruth, the ball sails true
beyond the left field fence. You tip your hat
"I told you so" with an expletive or two.

My Chicago-born wife, all fun no fret;
we have our World Series with no regrets.

Moreland, R.B. (2017) 2018 Wisconsin Poets' Calendar
"League of Her Own," page 44.

**Gerald George**
**Belfast, ME**

## O'er the Green Valley

They found out he could sing
so they pulled him out of the working prisoners
that they were guarding, told him,
"Sing a song, little rat."
It would pass the afternoon.

Full of fear, he felt he couldn't sing,
tears in his eyes, a choking in his throat,
but they were tenacious: "You will sing."
And so he sang, a cheery little tune,
despite the crying in his heart.

> *"O'er the green valley I rove, I rove,*
> *Until I shall find you my love,*
> *Waiting for me in the golden grove,*
> *Under the heavens above."*

"More!" the guards insisted, cheering,
so he sang another verse, then another,
all through the beautiful afternoon,
while the other prisoners kept on moving
bodies to the ovens for burning.

**Linda Shepard**
**Union, ME**

## Koan

The ferry pulls away from the dock.
The diesel smoke,
acrid yet comforting
mingles with the salt churned air.

The angled sun
sparkles the expansive sea.
A thousand light-tipped waves
carry me to this other shore.

Low tide air,
thick, ancient,
redolent with primordial memory,
layered with life and death,
I feel the stirrings of inexplicable joy.

The towering pines spiral upward,
intent on their conversations—
sky talk, bird talk, wind talk.
Their deep roots anchored and strong,
invisible to me,
yet I feel that earth pull
the downward search
wildly alive, nurtured, sustained.

Craggy rocks, smooth stones
the slowest heartbeat of all,
I listen in giant stillness for their one word
meant for me.

I come to the island to remember.
To remember my face before I was born.

**Charles Kaska**
**Heath Springs, SC**

## The Assignation

The lion picked up the wart hog's scent among the prints the kudus left when they scattered from the waterhole at first sight of him. The wart hog was not his first choice because of the bristly hair on its hide. But its scent was fresh and the kudus were now on a distant rise. He began his pursuit.

Paul and Cynthia Martin were the first to exit the van that had them, for the last three hours, from the Durban airport to the Phinda Reserve lodge. Cynthia was unsure of her footing because of a low grade fever. Paul steadied her on the step between the van's floor and the ground.

Rachel Carstairs exited without help and alone among the two other couples that comprised the van's passengers. The Martins were visiting the reserve to celebrate their wedding anniversary. Rachel had come to distance herself from the emotions of a recent civil—but no less painful—divorce.

The wart hog sniffed the ground frequently and the air occasionally but knew where she was going by sight. The Phinda cottages and the restaurant that fed their residents were less than two kilometers ahead. The trail was unfamiliar to the lion but it did not matter because the scent of the wart hog was like a series of guide posts and was getting stronger every minute. The lion padded on at a leisurely pace covering the same ground three times as fast as its quarry.

The Martins were worried about Cynthia's condition and were relieved when the resident physician assured them it was nothing more than a cold complicated by jet lag following the 12 hour flight from London. Nevertheless, she wanted Mrs. Martin to stay in the infirmary overnight in case the fever spiked. After a brief discussion they agreed and Paul left to fetch Cynthia's overnight bag.

The wart hog entered the compound from the southeast unobserved. She skirted the rearmost cottages and slipped under the wire fence that enclosed the garbage cans by shimmying on her belly. She walked to the nearest can and pushed off its lid with her snout. It hit the ground with a metallic sound that went unheard because of the noise in the kitchen. She sniffed and knew the contents would not be to her liking—too much curry. The second container held real promise: spoiled vegetables mixed with rancid meat. She tipped the can with her front hooves. It landed on its side with a dull thud and she began to dine. The lion arrived at the perimeter of the compound about the time the wart hog had eaten itself half way into the can.

Paul Martin and Rachel Carstairs had been shown to their respective cottages later than the other guests and by different attendants because they were at opposite sides of the compound. He had been delayed by the visit to the infirmary; she because she had stopped for a double Scotch on the rocks at the Safari Club bar. They both showered. Rachel changed into fresh clothes, examined her accommodations which were spacious and luxurious and walked to the dining room. Paul dozed for 20 minutes then dressed and did the same.

Rachel was already seated at a table set for four when he arrived. When she saw him scanning the room for a seat she motioned him over: "The dining room is crowded at this hour. You and your wife can join me if you like; I'm not expecting anyone."

"Thank you," replied Paul, "I saw you on the flight and we came in together on the van, didn't we?" Rachel confirmed his observations and motioned to the waiter. Paul ordered a Chardonnay, one of the South African varietals, like hers.

"Delightful!" exclaimed Rachel, "Does your wife drink Chardonnay? If she does we can order a magnum."

"She does," replied Paul, "but she won't be joining us. She's in the infirmary overnight."

Rachel's face darkened ever so slightly, "Nothing serious I hope."

**Charles Kaska**
**Heath Springs, SC**

"No. Just a cold and jet lag. But she's got a fever so they want to keep an eye on her."

"Oh I see. They're very attentive here. It makes you feel safe even if we are 'out in the bush' as they say."

"I'm Paul Martin, by the way. I guess we should introduce ourselves, don't you think?"

"I'm Rachel Carstairs. Pleased to know you."

She extended her hand. He took it and noted with admiration the carefully polished, perfectly manicured nails. Rachel saw his approval and was glad she had taken the opportunity to have them done at the Johannesburg Airport while waiting for the connecting flight to Durban. They interrupted their conversation long enough to order dinner—beef for him, fish for her—then reengaged immediately. After they exchanged the usual biographical information Rachel disclosed that she was divorced.

That news excited Paul and the excitement confused him. The beautiful woman sitting across from him was dressed casually but elegantly. Her hair style was relaxed and brushed against her bare shoulders, her makeup subtle. She knew how to converse and smiled beautifully. She knew how to attract and to engage men.

Paul's ten year marriage to Cynthia had not been unpleasant but nor did it have the excitement their courtship promised. That brief period was one of strong attraction and powerful sex. After the honeymoon they "settled in," as the expression goes, to a conjugal relationship and sex became routine. Cynthia no longer encouraged it and when Paul approached her she cooperated but without enthusiasm. They talked about having children but the time never seemed right given the demands of their respective careers.

By the time they finished dessert, a raspberry sorbet, an arrangement had been made: Paul would return to his cottage now while it was still light. Rachel would linger in the lounge for 15–20 minutes then walk down to cottage 34—his cottage. It was starting to get dark when she left.

**Charles Kaska**
**Heath Springs, SC**

The scent trail was undisturbed. In less than two minutes the lion's quarry was in view. His tail moved back and forth at the sight of it. He crouched so low that his belly was touching the ground and approached with short rapid steps. He took up position on the far side of the path that wound among the bushes that screened the kitchen from the cottages, and waited.

The wart hog finished slurping its exquisite repast and waddled slowly to the exit. She found it difficult to belly under the fence and scratched away some of the eroded earth. She was in the open now satisfied and a little sleepy. She ignored the impulse to settle under one of the bushes. Her burrow was the only safe place to spend the night. The lion observed it all from his vantage point.

Rachel stood on the elevated patio of the club house and looked out into the evening. She felt it would be awkward to ask an attendant to escort her to a cottage which was not hers. She could still see in the fading light and the lanterns along the pathway illuminated it sufficiently to make her way. She walked down. In a minute the path divided: hers to the right, his to the left. She removed her heels and padded along in her nylon clad feet making no audible sound. In another minute, perhaps two, she could make out the lights of cottage 34. She was relieved and realized that she had felt exposed and just a little intimidated in the unfamiliar surroundings. She walked on slowly but confidently.

The lion was up wind of the wart hog and downwind of Rachel. He did not hear her coming. She appeared from around a blind corner as he was about to start his ambush. He was startled and enraged that another creature would dare come between him and his prey. His hind legs unleashed their power and he was airborne. The wart hog screamed and was gone in an instant.

Paul Martin poured himself a double Scotch, drank it too quickly, lay on his bed and fell asleep. He awoke in the wee hours to use the bath room and realized Rachel was not

**Charles Kaska**
**Heath Springs, SC**

there, had never been there. He experienced a mixture of disappointment and relief. Sober and with a slight hangover he thought it was probably for the best. He drifted back to sleep.

In the morning he dressed and went to look in on his wife before breakfast. That's when he saw the notice tacked on the right side of the infirmary's entryway: "It is with profound sorrow and deep regret..." He read the rest mechanically without full comprehension. The final sentence refocused him: "Our guests are again respectfully reminded that under no circumstances should they move about after sun set without an armed escort."

Paul walked through the infirmary in a daze. Cynthia was sitting up in bed and smiling: "The fever broke about 2:00 a.m. I was able to get a good night's sleep and I feel great this morning. Did you miss me?" Paul forced a smile, leaned over the bed, took her in his arms and whispered, "You know I did." Neither noticed the tear that formed in the corner of his left eye then dropped noiselessly on to her pillow.

The wart hog made it back to her den without incident. Being the last one home she backed in as is the habit of her kind: Someone must keep an eye out for danger.

***

**Patrick T. Randolph**
**Lincoln, NE**

## Winter Path on the Farm

Horse tracks in the snow—
Frigid morning air—crisp breeze—
Rooster's crow starts Time;

Sun appears above the barn—
The horse still trots in warm dreams.

**Craig Sipe**
**Orr's Island, ME**

## deadheading last season's hydrangeas

stiff island winds
loft parchment
        tumbleweeds
over straw grass
the reaper
still dormant
after winter
        teeters on the stone wall
shivers like old wood
blown into new

***

**Thomas Peter Bennett**
**Silver Spring, MD**

## Doctor's Advice

Patient, be patient!
        Take a
tincture of time when
        impatience strikes,
until symptoms subside.

The recovery rate
        for patients with patience
is very high.

**Frances Henkel**
**Wauwatosa, WI**

## Close-Up

Fisted buds of peonies
show magenta promise.
Tiny, diligent ants
traverse tense roundness,
aid, abet floral surge to fullness.

Energetic jaws gnaw relentlessly.
Ragged edges release patient petals.
Former tightness explodes
into open hands of color and scent.

So unlikely this co-dependency
between insect and flower!
So obvious the benefit to the blossom!
So beautiful the outcome!

By what reckoning
does the ant know when and how
to undertake this labor of love?
What reward is there for the worker?

Was it an intoxicating quaff?
a super sweet dessert?
or mayhap, just the satisfaction
of a job well done?

Only the ants and the peonies know.

**Mary Jane Mason**
**Larchmont, NY**

## The Ballet Dancer

The sun begins its habitual descent
Shadows creep across the floor, darkening the salon
Dusky, gloomy, silent.
He dances on without the piano,
different music continuing on in his head,
propelling him around the room, tearing at his heart.

He clutches the dress to himself
her favorite costume, a silky, pink frock
holding it aloft, now spinning it around
now hugging it fiercely.
She is there with him
her feel, her scent, her presence
He aches.

The music, in a minor key, repeats hauntingly .
what is it?
He dances on and on, struggling to remember.
Street lights flick on. He remembers.
She'd told him gently, after rehearsing one day
of her leaving, of her failing body.
She would dance until the end and then go home.

Seeing her withered body in the sterile white bed,
her prediction now an albatross, a dark cloud
a nightmare.
And then it was over.
He'd been there, held her hand, watched as she relaxed,
        and slept

**Mary Jane Mason**
**Larchmont, NY**

He can't dream. She is present only when he dances.
Clinging to the costume now, his dancing slows
The room darkens. He sinks to the floor
and weeps.

***

**Jacob Fricke**
**Belfast, ME**

## Sky and Bait Knife

Hot August, a glossy night, ties and
black shirts on the footbridge to town,
the rods and lines and right there, holy on concrete, the
breathing squid—

a pile of eyes and luminescence,
opal tubes smacked silver dust,
some dim glass dunked in the murk of themselves,
regal jelly raw, here obscene against open air
and splotching black in angry scrawls, the pen's
spatter against the hatred of pavement,
the gravid dark, the bloated light;

*Look*, says the angle-man,
angling out the invert horizon,
his moonlight voice grainy, too murder-thin,
*over there now. See,*
*they're just like stars.*

**Anne Mullin**
**Bonita Springs, FL**

## Blue Tarps

Summer drivers would pass by
the brass bedsteads, rickety chairs
and bureaus that clung

to the embankment at that place
near Bath on northbound Route One.
We said we'd stop some day

when we weren't in a hurry to reach
our cabin two hours further north
or home two hours south

with four restive kids and two dogs
stashed with duffles and paddles and sleeping bags
in the back of the station wagon.

Sometimes we came up in winter when
blue tarps covered the lot, but in the last
several years we noticed

fewer covers flapping over the diminished spread.
We too were downsizing. There seemed
no reason to stop.

Yesterday you and I drove that stretch of old
Route One. We looked but we couldn't say
for sure where any of that past used to be.

**Rena Winters**
**Las Vegas, NV**

# Well-Behaved Women Seldom Make History in the United States

Consider for a moment that England, a monarchy, has managed to achieve outstanding women in history. Yet the United States which always considered itself as the most advanced democratic society ever, hasn't been able to elect a female leader in all of its independent existence so far.

Elizabeth 1 (1522–1603) was one of the most powerful English monarchs ever. Never Married and called the "Virgin Queen." The intellectual Elizabeth defeated the Spanish Armada and ruled successfully for so long that her reign from 1558 until 1603 is known as the "Elizabethan Era." As a monarch, the last of the Tudor Dynasty, she encouraged major cultural changes like the Renaissance and the transformation of England into a Protestant country.

Queen Victoria (1819–1901) was the queen of the United Kingdom, ruling over a vast British empire that stretched across six continents for 63 years. The second longest reign in its country's history (the longest belonging to the current Queen Elizabeth II). Queen Victoria the first's rule was so definitive that the period has come to be known as the "Victorian Era." Under her rule, slavery was abolished throughout all of the British colonies and voting rights were granted to British men. She also made reforms in labor conditions and presided over significant cultural, political and military changes in her empire.

Margaret Thatcher (1925–2013) was the Prime Minister of the United Kingdom between 1979 and 1990, the first woman to hold this office. She was the longest serving British Prime Minister of the 20th century, dubbed the "Iron Lady" by the Soviets for her hardheadedness. She won a popular victory over Argentina in the 1982 Falklands War, but her economic policies had mixed support, as she promoted a free

**Rena Winters**
**Las Vegas, NV**

market economy and confronted the power of the labor unions.

Now you better understand why I say, "Well-Behaved Women Seldom Make History in the United States." However, I do believe "the times they are a-changing for America."

For women, it's time they speak up and speak out about whatever concerns them.

We have to stop being victims and start being leaders.

When women and girls are empowered to participate fully in society, I believe everyone benefits.

***

**Sister Irene Zimmerman**
**Greenfield, WI**

## Poet's Plight

Thoughts, like sparrows,
dart in and out
of my mind.

How to catch them in mid-flight
without destroying
their exuberance...

Perhaps if I open the cage door wide,
they'll see that I don't intend
to pen them in,
but only to pen them.

**Peggy Trojan**
**Brule, WI**

## The Immigrant, 1906

Stoically shook Father's hand,
awkwardly embraced Mother,
boarded the train bound for Helsinki
and the boat.
Seventeen, on his way to America,
never to return,
or speak to his parents again.
Ship mail was slow, but they would write.

Minnesota held forests and lakes,
reminders of home.
Offered work on railroads
and lumber camps.
In his suitcase were some clothes,
a few photographs,
courage and determination.
He carried dreams by the handle.

Published in Talking Stick Volume XXI (2012) Honorable Mention

***

**Sylvia Little-Sweat**
**Wingate, NC**

## Bluet

Shallow breath of Spring—
softest blue, like Robin eggs—
crest on slender stem.

**Diane H. Schetky**
**Topsham, ME**

## Haiku Snapshots from Central America

**Waves**
Waves glow like little alps
        secrets lie below
only diving birds will know

**Cuba**
Amidst crowds and oppressive heat
      a little hand reaches out
the child is skin and bones

**Parasites**
Parasites eat at someone else's table
        too lazy to set their own
the cattle will be well groomed

**Fishermen**
Fishermen in a wee boat
        oh so far from home
will the Pacific stay so calm?

**Antigua, Guatemala**
Dusted with ash beneath
volcanos that never sleep
and rivers of lava that
have left their scars

**Nicaragua, Endangered Turtle**
She returns to her birthplace
        to lay 1000 eggs
the hungry poor will poach
        her if not her eggs

**Diane H. Schetky**
**Topsham, ME**

**Monstrous containers**
1000 colorful containers
boarding cargo ships
giraffe like cranes dangle
them about day and night

**Lake Gatun, Panama**
Bored sloth peeks out to
pose for a photo
ignoring howler monkeys

***

**Sally Belenardo**
**Branford, CT**

## Between

Between darkness and meager light
the cries of crows pronounce night dead,

and swift is my dream's demise,
between the last flying seconds of sleep

and the raucous caws waking my eyes
to a view between parted lace curtains

of wheeling crows and whirling snow,
of ebony wings plying the space between

obliterated sky and buried ground.
Drifting between the present and past,

I lie, frozen between choices to make
that I wish were as black and white.

**Andrea Suarez-Hill**
**Jonesboro, ME**

## Gratitude

November gale whips
inlet water white.
On eel grass geese harbor
'til storm retreats, their
creamy breasts like boats beached.

Parched snow coats
birch and fir trees
where iridescent ravens
await my Thanksgiving feed.
Rumps to wind,
horse and does paw
for snowfield's green
as an eight-point buck
snorts and sniffs unfazed
while I deliver hay.
Red fox scurry up the drive,
in pine tree turkeys hide.
A feral cat friend
arcs over barn door,
home at last
as gusts force
gray juncos to grass
beige plow scores.
Forest stewards all,
they welcome me outside,
a misfit toy
in Nature's sketch
who must aid
a planet on the edge.

**John T. Hagan**
**Springboro, OH**

## The Idea of a University

I'm getting old; I know it. All the signs are there. My road running times rival the fabled tortoise; my weight bench max-outs were once my warm-ups; I need three trips to the basement to remember the reason. You know, old.

Few of the harbingers of old age are more telling, however, than my grousing over the reasons why some young men and women attend, at least temporarily, their universities of choice. In his column in the *Dayton* (Ohio) *Daily News*, a staff writer characterized a University of Dayton basketball recruit's experience during a recent campus visit. Although the writer only repeated the recruit's list of U.D.'s strengths (all basketball related), I continue to be troubled by the dearth of references to the curricular reasons talented athletes cite for their college choices (you know, old).

As a retired, secondary teacher and administrator, I am increasingly concerned about the ostentatious events now trickling, no, cascading down from the collegiate level to high school athletics; such as, the National Kickoff Classic and the Flyin' to the Hoop extravaganzas. Organizers claim they are only showcasing young athletes (who actually could, in spite of the mendacity that denies it, obtain a college education without selling themselves to recruiters). The colleges, of course, become sycophants to the National Football and Basketball Leagues by running pro bono farm teams for franchise owners.

In my home state of Ohio, the reverence of the masses for The Ohio State University's football team exceeds any other form of state pride. This devotion is not in itself improper (perhaps mindless), but it seems to obscure or ignore the many glowing programs and merits of O.S.U. Most among the throngs who descend regularly upon the "The Shoe" on autumn afternoons could advise the neophyte attendee of the best places to park, the most delicious foods, or the best spirit attire to be found on campus. Many could also provide with encyclopedic accuracy the head coach's resume, the team's won-lost record against the opponent *du jour,* the starting lineups on offense and defense, the team's current national ranking, and maybe even who will dot the Script Ohio (a Buckeye State honor that ranks with the Nobel Prize). Ask those same zealots where to find the library, the School of Medicine, the School of Law, or the School of Agriculture, and they would likely tell you to consult a campus map. Ask them the national reputations of the magnificent Schools of Engineering, Arts and Science, Business, Nursing, Education, or Pharmacy; and many would scowl at you as some kind of crackpot or infidel. Travel the United States or abroad and ask the man-on-the-street (excuse my political incorrectness) what that person knows about The Ohio State University, and the answer would routinely be a reference to its legendary football team. This basis of recognition or identification is similar to Michigan State, Southern Cal, Penn State, Alabama, Florida State, or any other university with a football team perennially ranked in the top 25 nationally. Even those very selective schools such as Duke, Vanderbilt, Rice, Northwestern, Michigan, Stanford, and Notre Dame are known typically only for their football or basketball teams. (Okay, maybe not Rice.) Call me naïve or heretical, but there's something counter to the idea of a university about that.

As an undergrad majoring in English, I had foisted upon me at my small Catholic college the required reading (force-fed being more accurate) of John Henry Newman's *Apologia Pro Vita Sua*. Only the threat of its being the basis of an essay question on my future comprehensive exam (atypically required of undergrads at my college at the time) was sufficient reason for me to endure the tortures of Newman's protracted explanation for his switch from the Anglican to the Roman Church. Advice given but not taken was to fortify my

**John T. Hagan**
**Springboro, OH**

resolve with a fifth of Scotch while slogging through the murkiest prose. Newman was at the vanguard of the Oxford Movement (Tractarianism), and in a series of lectures, published collectively as *The Idea of a University*, he delineated what he saw as the mission of university life. Distilled down to its essence, the treatise maintains that grounding in general knowledge—a liberal education—is fundamental to any post-collegiate pursuit and that the purpose of a university is intellectual and pedagogical.

Intrigued by its title, many years after the strictures of my required readings, I read of my own volition *The Idea of a University*. While I was impressed by its depth and enlightened by its information, I was shocked by its being devoid of any reference to a university's mission to field national championship football teams. I found no reference to recruiting athletes for any sport or erecting arenas and stadiums that would accommodate thousands upon thousands of full-throated spectators. What glaring omission could exceed Newman's egregious shortsightedness! Did he not know that universities in America would one day be known almost exclusively for their enrollees' successes on the playing fields and courts? Did he not foresee that one day in America over 100,000 nearly delirious fans (many "adults" with painted faces and buckeye heads) would jam Ohio Stadium, nearly congealed into a mass of scarlet and gray, not to listen to readings from Cicero or Plato but to roar at one of the closest facsimiles to the Gladiators in the Roman Coliseum. How narrow-minded must Newman have been!

Make no mistake. I become as celebratory or vexed when watching my favorite college team on television as any of the most rabid fans in the stands. I am as swept up in the moment of a struggle between two national powers as anyone, and I have been known to throw a couch pillow when "my quarterback" throws an interception during the most critical play. When, however, in more lucid moments, I consider the disproportionate idolizations of the college kids who

**John T. Hagan**
**Springboro, OH**

labor primarily on the practice fields and courts to those who labor primarily in the libraries and laboratories, I question where we are headed as a society that venerates and compensates those who make first-down runs and three-point shots over those who may one day write the next exploratory expose (Ida B. Wells), invent the next breakthrough device (Thomas A. Edison), study the next endangered species (Jane M. Goodall), develop the next hybrid crop (George H. Shull), discover the next complex element (Marie S. Curie), design the next bascule bridge (Joseph B. Strauss), or find the next vaccines to "the thousand natural shocks the flesh is heir to" (Louis J. Pasteur). But hey, I'm getting old.

***

**P. C. Moorehead**
**North Lake, WI**

## Identity

A black rose in the radiant darkness
opened up and enfolded me.

I shivered in its midst.
Petal by petal, the rose fell.

Bare, I clung to the stem,
a black rose still, a radiant darkness yet.

Will I bloom again?
I do not know.

**Julie Babb**
**Damariscotta, ME**

## The Barn

It will not stand forever
This old weathered barn
That has leaned into storms
And cracked in summer sun.
Now home only to mice and bats,
It has been deemed useless,
An eyesore, something to be destroyed.
I hear the echoes
Of an impatient hoof knocking at the
Locked stable door.
A whinny, protesting a late breakfast.
The soft murmur of pigeon's wings
High up in the rafters.
A sunbeam gets caught in the motes
And I remember a whisper of warm breath
Upon my palm
Where the sugar cubes lay.

***

**Patrick T. Randolph**
**Lincoln, NE**

## Appreciating the Now

5 a.m.—first breath...
My wife in a peace-kissed sleep
I feel her dreaming;

Her eyelids flicker—I grin—
Glad I found her—years ago.

**Jerry James Rempp**
**Reasnor, IA**

## Nocturnal Verse

This evening
like so many other midnights
his mind immersed
in Beethoven, Chopin
and Puccini's
*Humming Chorus*:
Nocturnal ambiance insulating
a one-room universe

Sara Teasdale's lyrics
enchanting him:
*'Moon worn thin...'*
read at his father's funeral
His consoling legal pad
and pencil positioned to
unleash passion
gripping his soul this night

Not sufficient a wistful song
and plaintive verse
Night's specter emerges
calling him out-of-doors
Well he knows the appeal
and welcoming charge:
The starry depths
urging his zealous soul

To be under the influence
—fully high in wonder
Divinely cloaked and present
in many mansions

(continued)

**Jerry James Rempp**
**Reasnor, IA**

Consciousness in the all-in-One
—the One-in-all:
The creative vibrancy
in the nub of human design

He carries on, loosed
from every bit and piece
Composition quickening
against his strolling gait
The blazing universe
shooting star-filled designs
thru leaf-filled limbs
kindling burning wits

***

**Steve Troyanovich**
**Florence, NJ**

## the lost Siren

*y me guia a traves de la noche*
*la nina de la lampara azul.*
**—Jose Maria Eguren**

weaving this blue night
into the oblivion
of your blanketing song
my hands hold your shadow
where dreams remember dreams

**Robert Hodum**
**Sound Beach, NY**

## Coming In

Storm winds bring the sea tonight
Up over the cliffs,
Filtered through knotted clouds,
Down through fleshed-out maples,
And into this window.

The muffled-snare drum din of rain
On cottage roofs along the bluff
Deadens the breaking tide,
And it's eternal grinding of pebbles
And birthing of sand.

It's as if the Earth stopped spinning,
It's pendulum-like rhythms cast into a thundering vortex,
But down deep in antediluvian clay,
Unaware of this ship-wrecking gale,
its mantra persists.

"Life is eternal ..."

Pushing up through the depths,
Blithely carried ashore,
It resonates through mounds of kelp,
Scurrying horseshoe crab feet,
And frothed ocean,

" ... eternal."

Not till the gale slides east,
Leaving all eerily in silence,
Will the world's tilted whirl
And the cadence of its waves
Fill the night again.

**Gina Montini Mosca**
**Augusta, ME**

# Lost and Found

To love and be loved; this is all that my mother ever wanted. As I reflect on my mother's life and the 37 years I had the privilege of being loved by her, I believe she satisfactorily realized her inner heart's desire. For many women of my generation and the generations proceeding mine, this would not be merely enough. As a young woman, I struggled to understand how bearing seven children and sustaining a tumultuous marriage could coalesce into pure joy and personal life satisfaction.

My mother radiated pure love and joy. She had the ability to love family and neighbors alike unconditionally. Her heart offered others an open invitation for love and acceptance. She had the uncanny ability to make her seven children feel valuable and special in their own right. She enriched our bodies and souls with expressive affection, satisfying meals, warm blankets, individual tuck-ins, sing-a-longs, late night heart to heart talks, a loving presence during illness and guided prayer time. Her heart remained open despite mistreatment from others, marital conflict, the betrayal of friends, and tragic loss. Whatever tragedy occurred in our family, there is a secondary memory of my mother extending love, nurturing, and healing after the storm.

In family photos she was always glowing. She could be seen proudly holding one of her children, wrapped in the arms of her beloved husband, or sharing love and laughter with her sister and mother. Yet, as I grew older, I became keenly aware that beneath the smiles and laughter there were signs of hidden pain. A pain she silently drowned with alcohol.

I uncovered the mystery of my mother's pain when I discovered a tattered photo of her tucked away at the bottom of

**Gina Montini Mosca**
**Augusta, ME**

my grandmother's cedar chest. The photo was haunting. The sepia print was the only childhood photo I had ever seen of my mother. The photo depicted the likes of a lost pre-school child with golden pipe curls. She was long and lean and wore an undersized cotton hand-me down dress. Her brown leather shoes were tattered. She was standing sideways solitarily against a black back drop. Her crouching posture was tentative with knees bent like she could possibly be wishing she could run away or disappear. Her arms were tucked tightly against her body. In one hand she was clutching a naked baby doll. The other hand was fisted leading one to believe that she was distressed and guarded. As I looked at her face and into her eyes, I could not recognize the warm vibrant woman I had known. Her eyes appeared sullen and defeated. Her facial expression depicted suspicion and distrust. Her two lips were closed slightly, vacant of any expression of joy or happiness.

When I flipped the photo over there was a faded hand-written inscription: Nancy Duncan—Suwanee River Children's Home, Defuniak Springs, Florida 1935. Was my mother adopted, I wondered? In family folklore, my mother's dad died when she was an infant leaving my widowed grandmother with the challenge of raising two young daughters in the deep south, in the midst of The Great Depression. This photo, however, presented a different story. Why hadn't I heard it? In the 25 years that I knew my mother, you would think that this would come up. Then it came to my realization that this part of the family history was not shared for a reason.

As a Master's trained Social Worker, I used my professional skills to compassionately ask my mother about her past. In a heart-to-heart discussion she disclosed her real-truth. After the death of her father, my grandmother did her best to provide for her two young daughters on her meager salary as a telephone operator. Social Security and AFDC did not exist, so family and church were a widow's only support

**Gina Montini Mosca**
**Augusta, ME**

system. While my grandmother connected telephone lines, her children played on the property unattended. After my mother nearly drowned in the Tallahassee River, my grandmother's church stepped in. My mother and her older sister Peggy were sent to the church orphanage until my grandmother could get re-established. Many children at the orphanage prayed that someone would eventually come back to get them. This was the dream that fueled hope in my mother's young heart.

My mother and aunt spent ten years at the orphanage praying for redemption of their souls as strict religious dogma echoed their unworthiness. Corporal punishment was an acceptable form of discipline. My mother was beaten regularly for bed-wetting. She was separated from her sister Peggy due to age differences, but the bond of sisterly love sustained them. Compassion and altruism are often born through pain. After hearing the echoes of my mother's cries, her older sister Peggy would leave her unit in the middle of the night to toilet my mother regardless of the beating that awaited her when she returned.

When my mother was 12, she and Peggy were reunited with my grandmother. My grandmother had the means to support them, as she had married a respectable man with a consistent income. Alas, the story repeats itself two more times as my mother and her sister were subsequently abused by two step-fathers.

When my mother was 18, she met and married my father, a World War II naval veteran ten years her senior. My father was handsome, confident and protective—all the things she longed for in a man. Her desire for a loving protective father figure and a family of her own was her life's dream realized. Despite the pain of his alcoholic rages and associated violence, she loved my father dearly and never left him. She was a lost child and found security in belonging to someone.

My mother's greatest joy was found in the gift of motherhood and the creation of her own family. As a child, she had

**Gina Montini Mosca**
**Augusta, ME**

longed to be held and loved. She found this love in a rocking chair as she rocked her seven babies to sleep and fostered our growth and development.

Learning my mother's story provided great insight regarding her passivity and melted the anger I harbored regarding my own childhood wounds. She could have easily repeated the cycle of rage and abuse as a result of her past. Her resilience and ability to transform pain into joy, compassion and forgiveness was one of the greatest lessons she demonstrated to her children. Her legacy of love remains timeless.

My mother died 12 years after I learned her story. The last three years of her life bore witness to more pain and suffering as Alzheimer's Disease robbed her of her memory and abilities. She re-experienced the emotional distress of feeling lost in a world that she could not comprehend. She spent the last year of her life in a care facility, as she required 24 hour care. Despite her memory loss, she never forgot her children. Her face would light up whenever her children or grandchildren visited.

I had the honor of being with my mother as she took her last breath. As she crossed over from this life to the next, an unmistakable smile graced her face. I imagined her meeting her Maker, my father and other family members. The lost child was found once more.

**Sandy Conlon**
**Steamboat Springs, CO**

## The Perfect Crime*

To be shunned cuts deeper than a knife,
Is more precise, leaving no evidence to investigate,
Piercing the soul and closing all access to relief.

A bullet, a rope, some deadly elixir—
To such destruction doesn't begin to compare
Or touch the forlorn spirit left in its wake.

Death by shunning is wordless, complete,
Without repair or recourse to remedy.
Its weapons of silence and of distant space
Leave no blood or external signs of disgrace
And no access to human forgiveness.

*Some older societies have been known to use shunning against those members who openly sinned or broke the laws of the community. It is not known if the act is still widely practiced today.

***

**Genie Dailey**
**Jefferson, ME**

## Maine Spring

Twisted, wintry limbs
Reach out for springtime sunshine—
Soon, apple blossoms.

**Carol Altieri**
**Madison, CT**

## Lucca Biodynamica

In Tuscany, just beyond
the medieval walls,
country villas and pastures,
biodynamic vineyards flourish
free of chemicals,
in arcadian slope of greenery
where donkeys graze
in the labyrinth
of tangled paths.
Rosemary, lavender and rosebushes,
exhale bloom
intoxicating and pulling us in.

Wildflowers and white blossoming
olive trees blanket the terrain
in honey-colored gardens,
purple clover, golden mustard flowers
and crimson, wine vines,
a different dynamic way of growth.
The Lucca Biodynamica,
at center of all, Giuseppe Ferrua.
Swallows honeybees and plants thrive.

In 1735 Baroque Chateau
in sylvan hush,
we taste wines, made with natural yeasts,
that express their territory.
A deeper flavor
determined by heavenly bodies,
harvest under a full moon
mirroring the tides.

**Julie Babb**
**Damariscotta, ME**

## Requiem

The waves that carved the great cliffs of Dover
Will take the scattered bits of you
Over to the shore, on to the meadows.
Now filled with asters—
Catching the black-bird's eye
As if you were but a small black bug—
A tasty September snack.
While another, softer part of you
Soars upward,
Past my heart
Then gently
Downward
Sifts through my open fingers
With a whisper of farewell.......
I see you drifting lazy now, in and out,
In and out
Letting the ripples take you
Where they want you to go.
You
My lover of waves, of asters, of birds
Watcher of winds and tides,
Did you ever think that you could be
The waves that carved the great cliffs of Dover?

**Gordon Clark**
**Damariscotta, ME**

## Pool

The pool in the fall forest
deep, not cold but warm
warm against the chill of dusk
the indifferent day
I slip in, drink hot chocolate warmth
exhale, a slight moan
as I am infused
relax into an evening that breathes katsura
murmurs cricket song
Inhaling, listening, attending and yet not
I surrender to
this pleasure, this rest, this
dissolution of body and worries
Little will, less desire
to return to the fall forest

***

**Steve Troyanovich**
**Florence, NJ**

## eyes of stone...

*Like the abandoned moon, my lover.*
**—Youssef al-Sayigh**

mute worlds weep from another place...
wounded shadows stalk eternal emptiness
like the absence of warm moons...
words locked inside the threads
of their own loneliness...

**David Holt**
**Jacksonville, FL**

# Thanks, Dad

My dad would never have been called loquacious. However, he was very capable of expressing himself, and he did, when he thought he could add something pertinent to the conversation. He held in disdain those who he thought, “talked just to hear themselves talk,” so when he spoke to me I paid attention. A lot of his conversation with me tended to be instructive, and I usually heeded his advice, but no son, including me, ever did all the things his parents told him to do.

Dad was no raconteur, but he liked to laugh, and sometimes at our family dinner table he shared some of the cleaner jokes he heard from the men in the Maine Forestry Department. For example, “Why did Elvis hate the nick name, Elvis the Pelvis?”

“I don’t know. Why?”

“He had a brother named Eenis.”

Time with his family was important to Dad, in part because he was away in the Pacific during WWII, but also because when we kids were still small, for two years his job kept him away from home during the work week.

His preferred forms of recreation were active and outdoors—such as hiking, swimming or skiing—so we all participated in those activities. On hikes he would say, “Pretend you’re an Indian hunting for game. You’ll hear and see a lot more birds and animals if you are quiet. Watch where you step, and choose a rock or other hard surface. Don’t step on dead twigs that will break with a loud noise.”

He also had other woods’ lore, such as, “Branches that sweep across your clothing as you pass make noise—more so against nylon jackets than woolen. Avoid that noise by holding the branches aside as you pass. Human scent also alerts game to your presence. When possible, walk into the wind

**David Holt**
**Jacksonville, FL**

so that your scent will carry behind you and not scare the animals in front of you."

Dad expressed his care for Mom by encouraging us to take on age appropriate duties that would lighten Mom's workload. We learned to make our beds tucked in nice and tight—just like Dad had to do in the US Navy. We also could set and clear the table at a young age. After church when we kids were vying for the comics section of the *Portland Press Herald* we often would hear, "Why don't you help your mother get dinner on the table?" He promoted the concept that running a household is everyone's job.

Dad liked to be productive so it seemed that he always had some project in his basement shop. Before he left it at the end of the day he would always put his tools back in place and sweep up any debris. More than once I heard, "A good workman always cleans up after himself."

This need to be productive resulted in a decision to avoid the latest fad called television. I suspect that Dad and Mom waited until we were out of high school because they didn't want us to be distracted by it. They finally conceded that there might be some value in the "new" medium and they bought their first TV set in 1964.

Time and motion studies and efficiency were a big interest in the early twentieth century, and Dad grew up in that environment. I would hear things like, "Why make two trips, when you can do it in one?" "Let's look at your newspaper route to see how you can avoid backtracking." "You'll save yourself time and energy if you saw that branch straight across instead of on the diagonal."

Some lessons were a carry-over from his time in the US Navy. "You don't need to spend a lot of time in the shower. Just start at the top and work your way down. When you're finished, wring out your washcloth, and wipe yourself down with it before using the towel. Your towel won't get so wet and it'll dry faster.

When I began to shave Dad shared this, "Wash your face

**David Holt**
**Jacksonville, FL**

first. That will soften your beard. Then shaving will be easier." He also said, "I shave before bedtime because it saves me time in the morning and my beard doesn't grow much while I'm sleeping." Once when I mentioned I had to shave for my date that evening, he said with a smile, "I always do."

Dad's penchant for planning carried over to his driving. He passed along his driving tips that reinforced what I was learning in driver's education class.

"Look beyond the car right in front of you to prepare for possible contingencies. If there is a red light ahead, let your car's engine slow you down. By the time you get to the light it may change to green. You'll save wear and tear on your brakes and use less gasoline."

Although I had worked at summer jobs and for parts of the school year, when I was 21 Dad delivered me to my job as a bellhop on Cape Cod. His parting words were, "Before you get paid for more than you do, first you'll have to do more than you get paid for."

Thanks, Dad.

***

**Sylvia Little-Sweat**
**Wingate, NC**

## Daffodil

Golden trumpeter
blowing bold arpeggios
to bumble the bees.

**John Gillespie**
**Camden, ME**

## ten children, five lived to talk about it

face furrowed deep
with an ancient crop,
hair back hard in a bun,
but still a wisp or two refuse
and the eyes,
the eyes carry 85 years
in their photograph.

but it's the smile
that calls your bluff,
the toothless wrinkled smile
like an ocean licking rocks
until they are sand

and a wind blowing that sand
across Kansas into the eyes
of a girl boarding a train in 1917 Denver
and suddenly she starts to cry
and doesn't know why.

***

**Sylvia Little-Sweat**
**Wingate, NC**

## Front Porch

Early spring lilacs
scented breezes—like Grandma's
powder on my cheeks.

**Janice Babcock**
**Wauwatosa, WI**

## Memories Linger on My Finger

Traveling out of the country
I came back with jewelry
Memories linger on my finger

On my thirty-four-day South American cruise
Diamonds were not my intention
Lapis Lazuli was my love

Those native stones allured me
Shore excursion to Puerto Chacabuco, Chile
A surrounding village had only one good jeweler

That store was closed but I gazed through the window
I see many beautiful azure Lapis Lazuli pieces
I linger longingly looking at the Lapis inside

Finally the artisan owner returned
I found what I was looking for
A blazing blue Lapis stone set in a silver ring

The single ring was my exact size
Next, what was the price
My worried expression said it all

Owner calculated the cost in Chilean Pesos
Then equated to US dollars
We struck a deal

Now we both had smiles
And on my hand a blue Lapis Lazuli
Memories linger on my finger

**Hans Krichels**
**Bucksport, ME**

## A Tsunami of Turkeys

Good grief...
Working in my little treehouse retreat this morning,
And glancing out the window
Just then...
A flock of wild turkeys
Marching up the street,
Strutting their stuff
Now that Thanksgiving Day is behind them.
Strong image,
Those turkeys just outside my window.
Like all the deer under
The apple tree outback
Day after hunting season is over.
And just a few minutes later,
Roar of plow truck
Barreling down the street
Pushing a veritable
Slush-tsunami on its blade.
Probably got a few of those
Strutting turkeys.
Caught up in the mix.
Like deer jacked out of season,
Or those migrant families at the border,
Free at last
From the hardships at home
Dreaming of a safe future
In a new land,
Cut down instead
By tear gas at the crossing,
By separation from their children,
Watchful now for hunters

(continued)

**Hans Krichels**
**Bucksport, ME**

Out of season
And plow trucks bearing down
With side blades akimbo.

***

**Thomas Peter Bennett**
**Silver Spring, MD**

## Vocabulary Lesson

*—Alexander, age 4—*

Daddy!
Do you know what
Men witches are called?

What,
Alexander?
I queried.

Woodcocks!
He shouted.

No,
Alexander,
I coached:
Warlocks!

Ho! Ho!
He chortled,
Wearing his ski mask.

**Peggy Trojan**
**Brule, WI**

## West on I-40

On the way to California.
Miles and miles
of sand, rock, sage brush.
Looking out the window,
I saw them.

The man walking.
His gaze on the ground. Wondering
if he made the right decision.

The oxen, loyal, patient.
On the other side,
the boy and sister, missing friends.
Everyone thirsty.

The wagon. Huge. Like a boat
covered with grayed white sail.
Essentials. Cooking utensils,
dishes, clothes for the winter.
A stove. All they treasure.

The wife, following,
the bulge of the next child
large. Fearing the need
to stop, to bury it in the lonely sand.
Her bonnet faded pale
by relentless sun.
Her mother's teapot wrapped
in wool blankets, fragile
as hope.

**Juliana L'Heureux**
**Topsham, ME**

# Marble Steps to Maine

As a reporter who writes about Maine's Franco-Americans, my introduction goes like this: "Juliana L'Heureux writes about Franco-Americans but she's from Maryland." In other words, I'm not a Franco-American. Which, of course, begs the question of how I can write about a culture that's not my own?

Indeed, for the past 30 years I've been given the privilege to write at least one, sometimes two, stories every week about Franco-Americans. These articles are published in newspapers, journals, blogs and anthologies. Writing about Franco-Americans is interesting, because the culture is as diverse as the East Baltimore neighborhood where I grew up.

When growing up, I learned the value of family stories. Writing about Franco-Americans helped me to bind these stories with the cultures of my roots. Except, I've also learned how Franco-American stories are set apart from others. In fact, Franco-Americans haven't really melted into America's "melting pot." Instead, hard working French-Canadian immigrants were often more like itinerant laborers than immigrants. Yet, in other ways, I didn't see much difference between the cultural Franco-American stories and those I heard from a myriad of immigrant families, who were my neighbors in East Baltimore.

Maryland's founder was Lord Baltimore He requested the colony from the British Crown to serve as a haven for England's Roman Catholics, who were looking for religious freedom. Eventually, Baltimore City became a haven of hope for second and third generation European immigrant families. They settled in the growing city's eastern neighborhoods, a place where white marble steps were the pride of the all the doorways.

There were no shortages of trees Baltimore, when I grew

**Juliana L'Heureux**
**Topsham, ME**

up there. In the 1940s and 50s, carefully planted trees were spaced between row homes adorned with precision placed white marble steps, that extended into the horizon like a well crafted wall.

Patterson Park was adjacent to the row houses, lined up like soldiers at attention in the East Baltimore neighborhoods. The Park was a central refuge for the ethnically diverse urban dwellers.

As a matter of fact, a focal point of the park to this day is an unexpectedly lovely Pagoda, just like the kind a tourist would expect to see in Japan. This oasis brought out the best in the multi cultural neighbors, who often didn't even speak the same language

When I grew up in east Baltimore, our neighbors included Germans, Polish people, Italians, Sicilians (not to be confused with Italians), Russians, Ukranians and ethnic names I could hardly pronounce. Yet, almost everybody managed to got along! Perhaps Patterson Park was our green town hall. It was where children rolled down grassy hills and squirrels scrambled from tree to tree. As a matter of fact, Patterson Park, with its majestic pagoda, is still among Baltimore City's hidden treasures. It's literally located just across the concrete street from perfectly parallel rows of white marbled steps. Each set of sparkling white steps leads to the entry into a proud row home, usually a three story masonry house, decorated with painted window screens, depicting nature at its best, like waterfalls or stately swans swimming in clear ponds.

Built in 1890, the Pagoda has endured through decades of use and abuse. Although a structural curiosity, for those of us who grew up in its shadow, the pagoda was symbolic of vision. Although we were never allowed to climb to the top, we could imagine what it was like if we were looking at the world from up there.

Living on the second floor of one of those East Baltimore row homes, my mother often let me sit at the kitchen table to

**Juliana L'Heureux**
**Topsham, ME**

play with a very old fashioned toy typewriter. It wasn't a real typewriter, but it did type. A small central wheel pointed to a letter. Every letter was typed with great effort, as the typewriter ribbon was pressed by the corresponding key. "D-e-a-r N-o-n-a," my mother would say, as she then patiently waited for me to turn the little wheel to each letter she named. In fact, every week, I typed a letter to mail to my Italian Nona in Monesson, Pennsylvania. She loved my letters. They almost always started with "I am fine. How are you?"

These formative memories became my developmental stepping stones. Like the marble steps that led into my house and to those of all of my neighbors, these childhood memories also led to a realization about how writing could expand my horizons. Wow! I could communicate with Nona in Pennsylvania! Likewise, I could write to anybody, anywhere and at any time.

As a tribute to my mother, it should be evident to realize how the vision I anticipated while rolling beneath the grassy shadows on the Patterson Park Pagoda, was somehow infused into my little toy typewriter.

Writing about Franco-Americans is as gleeful an experience to me as typing a letter to Nona. Hopefully, my reports have contributed some sense of normalcy to Franco-Americans, who have not enjoyed the opportunity to take pride in their culture. While many history books hardly give French-Canadian immigrants any mention at all, the fact is, millions of patriotic Americans are Franco-Americans. Each person with Franco-American ancestry has a special story to tell to future generations. More often than not, the Franco-American family stories are ingrained in the threads of American history. Incredibly, most Americans are even unaware of how the French saved George Washington's American Revolution from disaster, before the victory at the Battle of Yorktown, VA.

Obviously, the vision I yearned to see from the top of the Pagoda helped to open my mind to the possibilities of life out-

**Juliana L'Heureux**
**Topsham, ME**

side of East Baltimore. Among the experiences I've enjoyed since leaving my home city has been a rewarding career as a professional registered nurse and a published writer.

My husband likes to say I've been a Franco-American for 50 years longer than I was the daughter in an Italian-Ukranian immigrant family, who lived in East Baltimore and then moved, even further east, to Dundalk, in Maryland.

Writing about Franco-Americans allowed me to tell personal immigrant stories. Like a cultural translating machine, the stories I've written are nearly the same ones I heard when growing up, but reported from a distinctly Franco-American point of view.

Those white marble steps that stretched out to the Baltimore horizon became the stepping stones to the American dream for many who shared my upbringing. Franco-Americans didn't always have the opportunity to step away from their tightly knit French neighborhoods.

Metaphorically speaking, the white marble steps eventually led me and my family to Maine, where I've been honored to write about my husband's Franco-American heritage. Although Franco-American history has been under-reported and, as a result, undervalued, my decades of covering the many aspects of the group's identity has, hopefully, helped to instill pride in the culture, that predates the founding of America.

**Patrick T. Randolph**
**Lincoln, NE**

## The Guardians

Midwestern farmers
Define this country's spirit—
Their souls are our souls:

Their lives create this sweet land,
This sweet land creates our lives.

***

**Linda Shepard**
**Union, ME**

## No Guru Needed

A walk in the woods today,
a desire to fill myself with November's calm,
gray sky, brown ground, the old pines' deep green.
Climbing the hill
I am given gifts.
Crow song, a piece of quartz,
a pod I do not recognize,
my pant cuffs burr studded.

I descend emptying.
My thoughts, trailing behind me
dissolve like vapor.
The quiet stream winds beside the path,
a soft song bubbling over smooth stones.
I arrive at the bottom of the hill
a hollowed being.
Dipping my hands in icy water, anointed.

**Sally Belenardo**
**Branford, CT**

## Fatal Statistic

Stopped in traffic
she waits

in a rush, one hand
holding the wheel,

the other
a cigarette,

her face
framed by curls

of smoke,
her lips puckered

in another kiss
of death.

**Gerald George**
**Belfast, ME**

## Flowers Await

*In memory of Ilse Weber, a Jewish songwriter from Prague, who sang to children as she went with them into an Auschwitz gas chamber in 1944.*

*Lullaby, lullaby, I am right here beside you.*
Her voice melodious, gentle, and clear.
*Be brave little children. Come into the room.*
How could they hate these young ones so dear?
*Of the flowers that bloom in the summer we'll sing,*
*your pretty eyes close. See the sweet joy they bring.*
*Come my little ones, come.*

The children come to her, gathering around.
*The sun casts its rays on the tiniest being.*
She just keeps on singing, her words are like balm.
*Let lovely sweet flowers be all you are seeing.*
So soothing her voice, though her eyes fight the tears,
she lovingly holds them to quiet their fears.
*Calm my little ones, calm.*

*Lullaby, lullaby, you will soon be at peace.*
She holds them so tightly as she sees the chamber.
*Don't open your eyes, O dear ones, don't peek.*
The sound of the gas begins as they enter.
*Now flowers await you, so tranquil, so still,*
*the flowers that love you, as always they will.*
*Sleep my little ones, sleep.*
*Sleep my little ones, sleep.*

**E. M. Barsalou**
**Kittery Point, ME**

## In a Wooded Abandon

Above a cold grey sky—
The lone crow glides
Through a narrow crest
of hefty tree line-cawing.
Seeking meal or shelter
rampantly aloft; dovish.
A storm front which descends
In a whiter shade of pale
On the brow of hidden blue
In the horizon towards a sunken
watershed beneath the valley below.
The trail between its overgrowth
Of fallen arbor—this forest
denouncing its own life;
that hath once grown stronger.
Tapering along a lake's inlet
Around fresh shoreline
Almost its slithy-toves and
Maple groves, covered by
A winter's blanket, that showers
Down in constant pindrops of
Hail and snow—calmly accepting itself.
No one knew of its encounters,
Its mass that adamantly surely shows
Of loneliness and woes—torturous
With memories of seasons past-by.
Those I had never known,
In a wooded abandon.....wise.

**Steve Miller**
**Islesboro, ME**

# Glow

The warmth from the fire in the cookstove is obvious, tangible—chunks of beech and ash, kindled to flame from match and dry cedar, morph to red coals that throb with intensity. Heat you enter in a field near the stove, its ardor on your fingertips as you slowly move your hand just inches over the cast iron top.

But there is a warmth in this house that's greater than the Glenwood's radiance. The honeyed sunlight of this cinnamon toast December morning sweetens the air, too, the full depth of the house, front to back. Can wood—pine and spruce boards and timbers, their natural colors benevolent in this buttered gloss—can wood heighten the warmth I feel? Is this contribution real or imagined? Can the house warm itself?

Then Pippen, asleep on the back of grandfather chair, stretches, yawns, and curls his paws under his dandelion down and striped fur, simultaneously adding to and drawing from the comfortable house.

Stepping out into the cold that makes rocks of mud and dirt, then back inside to the occasional pop and swish coming from the stove, the sweep of warmth against cherried cheeks, the fragrance of fresh black coffee dark as fir trees on moonless nights, a childhood rush of joy and inspiration arises—from where? These perceptions of now—so mingled with yesterday and tomorrow—perhaps seed flame? I think this house has itself become a generator of heat, a source of belonging and love, a living, breathing Being ready to welcome kindred souls.

Or maybe the warmth is all inside, blush of blood and flash of desire, a heart, this moment like a brilliant crystal, radiating warmth to air and surface, timber and plank, kiln and little mammal. I don't know. I may never know. And today, in the golden glow, it does not matter at all.

**Robert B. Moreland**
**Pleasant Prairie, WI**

## Senior Prom

Oh God she prayed, make me radiant, bright;
I am short of stature, freckles imbued.
Thankful for long auburn hair to hide sight
of one, in my own eyes, homely and crude.
With trim little waist, keen mind's attitude,
why would anyone want to dance with me?
This corner is dark, I'll watch all I see;
love is not for bookworms or plain short girls.
She sat demurely, in shadows shyly,
love as far away as all the lost worlds.

In black horn-rimmed glasses, with all his might,
class genius par nerd, jocks are always rude.
They will use you when the answers are right,
tossing you off as outcast, comments lewd.
Took all of his courage, tried to be shrewd;
come to his only senior prom and be
one who could dance with some brightest filly
arrayed in long cerulean gown, pearls.
For his heart beat as theirs did, not silly,
looked across the room to spy her lost worlds.

Trembling voice, he asks her to dance this night.
She smiles, for the first time sees him, renewed.
Womanly form, blue gown decked pearls, moonlight;
waltz around parquet, their eyes meeting trued.
Confidence gaining, comes into their view,
Strauss strains ending, he bows then she curtsies.
They sit, enraptured, discuss Emily...
for this, cerebral bliss, highest plain whorls;
opinions flying, her eyes filled with glee,
Columbus has discovered the New World!

**Robert B. Moreland**
**Pleasant Prairie, WI**

Creation of minds, sweet reality,
born of two so in tune, veracity!
Moonlight gleams off each alabaster pearl,
noses collide, first kiss now history;
beauty in a fresh light, a brave new world.

***

**Peggy Trojan**
**Brule, WI**

## Autumn

The aspen leaves
are a gold flutter
in the wind
as they prepare to fly
in a last grand swirl
of dance.
I watch them
in wonder every autumn,
marveling
at their beauty
and their willingness
to accept the cycle
of their short lives.

I imagine
the letting go,
and the dance.

Published in *Ariel Anthology 2018*

**Sister Irene Zimmerman**
**Greenfield, WI**

## Debut

Though winter keeps
a stranglehold
on field and creek,

crocuses have sliced
through crusts of snow,
and pussy willows

bloom with birds
that serenade
budding debutantes.

***

**Steve Troyanovich**
**Florence, NJ**

## the orphaned do not dream...

*But the voice of the wind I could understand.*
**—Anna Akhmatova**

across these sweeping drifts
the wind plays nocturnal flute...
memory ices its weeping gaze
now mingled with absent voices...
there loneliness stood
alone mourning the solitude
of an orphaned snowman

**Judy O'Dell**
**Rockport, ME**

## Working Eight to Five

Only those of a certain age might remember working at a gray metal desk with its expansive, clean surface. No looming computer monitors. A pencil drawer, not keyboard tray, bridges two columns of drawers that trap heat in the summer and radiate cold in the winter. The narrow chair opening would force your feet to rest flat on the floor, assuming the chair is adjustable to your height. I am watching the 1940 Preston Sturges movie *Christmas in July*. The main character works in an office where there are rows upon rows of metal desks, each occupied by a man in a light-colored suit jacket. What they are doing is unclear. The boss, in a dark suit, roams the room, figuratively cracking a whip. I have a sudden flashback to September 1970.

I am a newly married, recent college graduate with an accounting degree and ambition to become a certified public accountant. I have moved to Des Moines, Iowa, where my husband has started medical school. I've sent resumes and answered ads. It seems that no CPA firm in Des Moines wants a woman on their professional staff. The wedding cash is running out, and there is rent to pay. I sign on with a temp agency. They call me a few days later, saying this might not be what I had in mind, but the company, Massey Ferguson, needs help. Think red farm tractors. On my first day, I dress in my job interview suit and ride downtown with my husband. The company's office is on the third floor of an old office building. I introduce myself to Betty, the receptionist, and we chat for a few minutes. She grows suddenly silent as a small man about forty years old, dressed in a dark suit, comes out to greet me. His name is Mr. Burdess.

Mr. Burdess escorts me to a large room with tall windows facing the street. It is filled with rows upon rows of gray metal desks occupied by women of various ages clacking away at

**Judy O'Dell**
**Rockport, ME**

adding machines. My desk is in the center of the room facing a white column. Mounted on the column is a black rimmed clock. The only item on the scratched gray surface of the desk is a green Burroughs ten-key adding machine.

"The company is in the process of converting its billing to a computer system," Mr. Burdess explains. "Invoices to all of our dealers are sent here." He pulls one out from the large cardboard box sitting beside the desk and continues, "On each invoice are the part number, quantity, and price. Your job is to multiply the quantity by the price, then add up the totals. You do know how to use an adding machine?" I say yes even though the only one I ever used was in my father's office where I occasionally checked the math on my accounting homework.

"The workday is 8 to 5; there are 15-minute breaks at 10 and 2. Lunch is an hour from 12 to 1. Frances will sit with you this morning to show you the ropes." With that, he goes back to strolling around the room. Frances is a small woman, about forty, with permed blond hair and a pleasant smile. "Let's get started," she says. "I'll introduce you to some of the girls at break time. The ladies room is down the hall if you need it."

We pull the first invoice from the box. The dealer's name and address is printed under the Massey Ferguson logo. There are columns for quantity, part number, price, and total. Then, handwritten, six items are listed. The first line reads Quantity 7, Part Number M2758590, Price $3.47. I type in 3.47 on the machine and hit the repeat key seven times. The result is $24.29 which I write in the total column. I do the same with the other six items, total them and write $179.52 neatly at the bottom of the invoice.

"That's all there is to it," Frances says, and I pull the next invoice from the box. She watches as I peck at the adding machine.

"Look," she says," you have to get faster. Think of the adding machine like a typewriter. Put your index, middle and ring fingers on the 4, 5 and 6 keys. Feel the bump on the 5 key? That lets you know where you are. Your index finger does 1, 4, 7; your middle finger does 2, 5, 8, and your ring finger does 3, 6, 9. Your thumb handles the repeat key marked with an X. Your little finger hits the large plus key and moves up to hit the total key. Now look at the number on the invoice and think about where your fingers are. Don't look at the machine. Type in 45.39."

I mentally picture the keyboard, place my fingers on 4, 5, 6 and think hard about 3 and 9. I end up with 45.93 on the tape. I try again, and this time I get the number right.

"Mr. Burdess will cut you some slack for your first few days; then he'll be on you to get faster. So, practice touch adding. I've been here for five years, and it took me only a few days to learn it."

Mr. Burdess stops at my desk. "How's it going?"

"Just fine" I answer. "Frances is very helpful." As he walks away, she glares at his back. I begin to wonder about the dynamics in this office.

I spend the rest of the morning practicing touch adding. I check the tape before writing the amounts on the invoice. At break time Frances introduces me to several of her friends who are permanent employees. Processing the invoices is a special project which requires about ten temps like me. At noon a beautiful dark-haired woman, about my age and very pregnant, comes to my desk. "Hi, I'm Susan. How about lunch?" she asks. "There's an inexpensive cafe around the corner." I nod and grab my purse.

Over BLTs and Cokes, she asks if I'm a college graduate. I am puzzled by the question, but nod yes. She continues, "I'm the only college graduate in our office, and I could tell by the way you're dressed that you probably are one too. I was teaching third grade, but once I became pregnant and started to show, I was not allowed in the classroom. I'm just doing this until the baby is born."

I tell her that I have been married for just a month, that

my husband is engrossed in his school work, that I miss my family and friends in Philadelphia and that I'm having a hard time finding a job. I have my first friend in Des Moines.

The afternoon wears on. It seems as though the little hand on the clock will never to get five. Mr. Burdess occasionally checks on me and nods as he makes his rounds. He breaks up a conversation between two women in the back of the room and then another by the restroom. I wonder what he does when he is in his office. The only sounds in the room are the rotating wheels on the adding machines and the occasional clang of metal desk drawers closing. Five o'clock arrives. The office is empty by 5:02.

"How did it go? my husband asks when I meet him at the college parking lot.

"Well," I answer, "I did not need to go to college to do this."

He smiles at me and says, "It will be worth it someday."

"I hope so," I sigh. We discuss what to have for dinner.

The days wear on. I dress like the other women, wearing my old college wardrobe of skirts and blouses. Boxes of invoices are piling up at the front of the room. Mr. Burdess roams the room, up one aisle and down the other. To alleviate boredom, I start timing myself. How many can I do in five minutes? Can I do twenty invoices in seven minutes? What are these parts anyhow? Where do they fit in a tractor? Why is this one so expensive? Is Mr. Burdess bored too? He is the only man in the office.

Going to the ladies' room is another way to break up the day. I learn that Mary Jane was married before she finished high school. I learn that Barbara, who is my age, has three children whom her mother cares for during the day. I learn that Linda is a grandmother at age thirty-five. I learn that Kathy gets up at 4 AM to help her husband with farm chores before coming to work. I learn that Nancy's black eye doesn't necessarily mean she walked into a door. I learn that Frances won a blue ribbon for her rhubarb cake at the state fair. I learn that information is freely shared and overheard in an office ladies' room. I learn that life in the real world is hard. I learn to respect and care about these women. Mr. Burdess periodically knocks on the ladies' room door to remind us it is not break time.

One day he comes to my desk to tell me he is impressed with my speed and accuracy. My job will change. From now on I will be checking the invoices processed by the others. If it is tedious to add up the invoices, it is even more tedious to check them. I start keeping statistics on how many errors there are in a stack of 25. Could I check a hundred in 30 minutes? The little hand on the clock seems to move more slowly. Susan does not show up for work one morning. Betty reports that she is in labor. Later that afternoon we learn it is a boy. I lose my lunch companion.

At night I scan the want ads and send unsolicited resumes. I know the firms will be staffing up for the busy season soon. Finally, I get a call from a local CPA firm and arrange for an interview after work. There are three partners and four staff. It's not Arthur Young, the Big 8 accounting firm that made me an offer before graduation in Philadelphia, but it is a start. I am hired for $550 a month. It covers our $149 a month rent, and I will be gaining the required one year of experience towards my CPA license. I finish out the week at Massey Ferguson, and on Friday morning I inform Mr. Burdess that I will not be back. "I'm sorry to see you go, Judy.

I am not sorry, but I remember advice from a wise old nun who told me "never burn bridges." I smile and say "Thank you for the opportunity, Mr. Burdess."

At afternoon break, my co-workers give me going away party. We all hug and I promise to stay in touch.

On my second day at the CPA firm, Ben, one of the partners, and I drive thirty-five miles to Winterset, Iowa to start a bank audit. He tells me that John Wayne was born there and points out some covered bridges as we drive through

**Judy O'Dell**
**Rockport, ME**

Madison County. Farmers and Merchants State Bank sits on one corner of the town square. The bank president greets us and shows us to the conference room where we will be working and, more important, the location of the coffee pot.

The bank's records are not computerized. On the table is a green ten-key adding machine, a black general ledger and a two-foot-long metal tray of ledger cards, one for each customer, which tracks his/her bank balance. Ben instructs me to add the balances at September 30. My right-hand flies over the adding machine as I flip through the cards with my left. My little finger hits the total button after the last card, and I hand him the tape. It agrees with the general ledger to the penny. He looks at me in amazement. "How did you do that so fast?"

"Lots of practice," I answer with a smile. The workday passes very quickly.

**Frances Henkel**
**Wauwatosa, WI**

## a seeker of silence am I

*a seeker of silence am I*
**—Kahlil Gibran**

a seeker of silence am I

in the starlit night sky
in the moon as it runs its course
in the balm of a sun-full day
in the breath of a gentle breeze;

*a seeker of silence*

in the fragrance of spring flowers
in the scent of new-mown grass
in the incense of burning leaves
in the hushed fall of clinging snow;

*a seeker*

in a dreamless night of sleep
in the stillness of pen on paper
in the quiet reading of a poem
in the peaceful praying of the Psalms;

*a seeker am I*

in the presence of my God
in the protection of my angel
in the company of dear friends
in the depth of my inner self;

*a seeker of silence am I*

in the warm embrace
        of a loved one.

**Sylvia Little-Sweat**
**Wingate, NC**

## Conversation at Autumn Care

Past one hundred, Mrs. Bertha can
no longer hear it rain nor thunder,
but by squinting still can read
card-size sheets for conversation.
*You are so pretty*, I write. *Thank
you,* she bellows for in her world
there is no sound of words, only
the way they feel in her throat.

I write my name on another page
and claim the woman to my right
as Mother and then acknowledge
Mrs. Bertha's age and quip that she
*makes Mother at ninety-one a teen.*
She chuckles, pleased at the joke
at her expense. Age is all she has.
She reads more of my small talk.

Jealous, Mother reaches for the page—
listening in—to our conversation. Your
*mother is a pretty woman*, she utters.
I smile a thank you from both of us.
*Would you like for me to take the sheets
to your room for later*? Another nod,
and I am off to place the letter beside
her bed. She waits to eat her cake.

*Do I leave now*? she asks loudly. I nod,
*Yes ma'am* and wheel her back down
the hall to her room then visit Mother.
Before leaving I walk the hall again. I

(continued)

**Sylvia Little-Sweat**
**Wingate, NC**

see Mrs. Bertha still in her wheelchair,
her back to me, hunched over the
penciled sheets—like an old, old crow—
pecking the pebbled words for gold.

***

**Bob Whitmire**
**Round Pond, ME**

## Hymn to Endings

Fie on the never ending sky
The feckless sparkles on the sea
The selfish arrogance of gulls
The sodden tracks that follow me

Along the windy stretch of beach
My toes find every sharpened shell
My face turns always to the sun
That winks and proffers hints of Hell

The water takes on restless churn
Unseen the hidden riptides flow
They hum the hymn, the end of me
The breeze, the sun, the sand a'glow

I laugh and turn, run up the dune
And watch the sun drop to its doom.

**Bob Whitmire**
**Round Pond, ME**

## Waiting Room, Togus

*Veterans Administration Medical Center*

Old birds, tired feathers,
too many flights
too many fights,
wait on their wires
until the sweet doves
call them back
for healing remedies.

Prognoses aren't good,
ages too advanced
wounds too deep
not enough feathers
left to fly
but all of them try,
tumble from their wires—

squadrons of crows
sweep in to carry
them across
the widest of rivers,
set them lightly down
on cool grass under
a bright sky where
no sun shines
and no rain falls
and the breeze
wafts soft and warm.

**Bob Whitmire**
**Round Pond, ME**

I wait on my wire
for the doves to call
and pray the crows
don't come
for me today.

***

**Robert B. Moreland**
**Pleasant Prairie, WI**

## Seeking Substance

In the August of life, we think we still
have time to spare; warm summer's seduction
whispering immortality. We fill
each moment with busy and production

all the while breathlessly immediate
(but not important) boxes checked, fires quelled.
A tapestry woven, patterns satiate
who we are until we are but a shell?

Age like a thief in the night steals away
ability to take advantage of
living to the fullest each and every day;
satisfaction crowned with love.

With retirement, discarded and songs sung;
too late realize youth is wasted on the young

**Anne Mullin**
**Bonita Springs, FL**

## Seasonal

We drive by the swamp rimmed
with all the gold and bronze and
crimson of the season, where
a couple of pale skeletons of pines
raise bleached appeals to a sky
that was blue yesterday.

Today leaves are falling under
heavy rain, skittering sideways
as if refusing to come straight down,
like the way we used to walk
the off-beat way home from school
through an abandoned gravel pit

where chicory and burdock grew
and trees were sparse. Sometimes
we would find under scuffed leaves
at our feet a horse chestnut
missed by the bigger kids who
hoarded them for pelting us later.

Past moments appear at random
in our vision like the occasional
yellow leaf sluicing off the windshield
now, like the surprise of dead trees
that endure in morbid contrast to
this seasonal riot.

**Georgette Carignan**
**Limerick, ME**

# The Island Way

Dying, like living, on a remote island in Maine presents certain challenges. On this October day, the sun was shining and the water sparkled. From the mail boat, Savannah could see about 10 islanders milling about on the dock. Some were there for no other reason than to watch the mail boat come in, it was a ritual of sorts. Others were hoping for packages and supplies. Ev Spear was there to meet his granddaughter and stand his ground. Neither cancer, nor an insistent granddaughter, was going to get Ev off the island, only God would do that in His own good time.

Savannah had always had mixed feelings about the place but no one could deny the wild beauty that was Stag Island, the cliffs, the surf, the crazy colorful sunrises and sunsets, the dark reaching spruce trees, the isolated and fragrant hiking trails. But then there was the town, with its dusty antique hotel, its one church, the weather beaten store, Loretta's Coffee Shop (a converted front porch). To Savannah, it wasn't quaint or charming; it was airless.

The lifeblood of the island, the dock, was busy with fishing boats and dinghies. The mail boat came twice a week with the occasional tourist (at least in summer). In winter the rare "tourist" consisted of runaways of one form or another, writers working on their prize winning novel (the island had yet to produce a best-seller or even a published book for that matter), and the depressed, looking to run away from civilization. Mostly they would go back on the very next mail boat, a little more depressed, a little more lonely and disillusioned but grateful for plowed roads and reliable electricity.

Savannah was relieved to see that Ev looked well, very tan, a bit thinner than the last time she'd seen him, but not alarmingly so. He had always had that craggy unshaven Clint Eastwood look about him.

**Georgette Carignan**
**Limerick, ME**

He helped her with her suitcase and gave her a hug. "Good to see you."

"Nice to see *you*!" *alive* she thought.

"You didn't have to come, you know," he said.

"I know, I wanted to come."

Her wheeled suitcase bounced and tilted out of control on the cobblestones from the dock. The island had no roads, they were essentially wide paths intersected with tree roots. Cars and bikes were equally useless. For moving goods and people, it was golf carts and one of the two ATV's on the island.

Savannah and Ev walked to his cottage just beyond the village center. She did notice that he was winded when they arrived and that he was relieved to reach a kitchen chair and sit down. When he saw her expression he smiled patiently.

"It's okay," he paused. "*And*, for the record, I am not going back with you."

There were never a lot of preliminaries between them. They always went straight to the point and in that way they were alike.

"There would be resources that you don't have here. I could help you with things – groceries, getting prescriptions, seeing the doctor," she said.

"Savannah," he patted her hand. "I'm an old man. I'm 84. I came to this island 30 years ago, I'm not leaving." It was a statement of fact; he was not building a case.

She sighed and looked up and noticed that the kitchen was clean. There was a Mason jar of wild asters on the table and a plate of blueberry muffins in plastic wrap. Even his paints and canvasses were at least contained in a corner of the room. It was surprising as housekeeping had never been a priority for Ev.

The island was a magnet for the heartier of artists and Ev caught the bug to paint shortly after his arrival. He never took it seriously and in fact he wasn't very good. His pictures were rather garish and somewhat primitive. Nevertheless he sold an occasional canvas to a tourist who would happen upon him on the back shore while he was painting or someone would see one of his pictures hanging in the store.

His actual income came from his early retirement benefit, social security when it kicked in, and various odd jobs and services. And, most importantly, Ev was gifted with the ability to survive on almost nothing. He considered today's consumerism a national tragedy.

"Where did these come from?" Savannah asked indicating the muffins.

"Lilly. I told her you were coming."

Savannah bit her lower lip remembering Lilly from her last visit, two summers ago, an energetic, talkative, powerhouse of a woman with a thick Maine accent, a rather mannish haircut and passionate about gardening and sailing and fishing. She never seemed to sit still. Savannah hadn't realized they were friends, at least not close friends. And apparently she bakes!

As if on cue, Lilly rapped loudly on the door.

"Yoo-hoo, anybody home? Well hi there, Savannah. You haven't had any of the muffins yet? They're good. Made 'em this morning. Here, I'll make some coffee."

Savannah felt a little disoriented. Her grandfather was a loner (another trait they shared). That's why he had left his job at the paper, that and grief after Savannah's grandmother died.

Lilly appeared very comfortable in her grandfather's kitchen bustling about. The worst thing was that her grandfather actually looked relieved! She chastised herself for being so juvenile and made herself enjoy the muffins and promised herself a run on the back shore.

"How long you staying for, honey?" Lilly asked.

"I don't know...it depends." She looked at her grandfather who had taken only a small bite of his muffin.

"She thinks she can wear me down. She thinks I will go back to Boston with her." He winked at Savannah who had to acquiesce.

The family tree was small to start with, an only child born to an only child, add to that the vagaries of life, and Savannah's divorce....

"Grandpa, it's just the two of us," she sounded whinier than she intended. "I don't want you to be alone, I want to help you."

Lilly was humming quietly as she rinsed dishes in the sink.

"I will leave you two alone now," Lilly said, and she was gone leaving the cottage smelling of coffee and baked goods.

"Why don't you go for your run. We can talk when you come back," Ev said. He looked exhausted and was eyeing the couch.

When she got back, Ev was still asleep. She watched his breathing for a few moments and saw how really sunken his cheeks had become, and was reminded of the last days and weeks of her mother's illness.

Over breakfast the next day, they addressed Savannah's "mission."

"Listen, Grandpa, I've taken a family leave from work. Twelve weeks. If you come to Boston we can be like roomies. We can go to museums, and movies..."

"Twelve weeks, so that's how long you think I have."

Savannah rubbed her eyes, "No, that's how long I have—of leave time."

"How about a compromise, we can be roomies here on the island."

Savannah rolled her eyes. "You're going to need things. Medicine... a doctor. Your doctor is a two hour boat trip away. *This* doesn't make any sense," she said looking around the room.

"I'm staying here. A hospice nurse has already come out to see me."

Savannah's mouth went dry. Of course she knew how serious it was, but to have it verbalized felt like a punch in the stomach. "Does hospice come out here?" she asked in a weak voice.

"I told her not to come back," Ev said. There was no indication of anger or fear in his voice.

He reached into a cabinet and took out an envelope that was propped between the mismatched coffee mugs. "Here is what I want. I wrote it all down. I want to be buried at sea." He paused. Savannah felt like she couldn't breathe. She started to open the envelope. "Not now. Read it when you have a minute." She stopped fumbling with the envelope and blinked back tears.

He looked into her eyes and squeezed her hand. "We can do this." Then his eyes brightened. "Tonight, meatloaf at Loretta's! On me!"

Savannah didn't know if she should laugh or cry, but she agreed to staying on the island and the meatloaf.

She caught the next mail boat and went back to Boston. She made arrangements with someone to check on her apartment once a week, packed boots, warmer clothes and more underwear and once again boarded the mail boat for Stag Island and watched the mainland recede.

When she got up the courage to read what was in the envelope, Savannah was taken aback. She was prepared to read that he wanted help with suicide at the very end, (not that she was keen on that, either) and certainly he would not be amenable to life support... but no, none of those issues were addressed. The letter simply stated that he was going to stay on the island and when he passed he wanted to be taken out on Justin Lewis' lobster boat and dropped into the sea. The letter ended by stating that it was his, Everett Spear's, final wish and decree.

*Is that even legal*, she thought; *I don't think you can just dump a body in the ocean.*

It wasn't long before they settled into a comfortable routine. For Savannah it was breakfast, a run, chores. Ev ate little and napped a lot. He put effort into maintaining his routine, which was coffee at Loretta's with his island cronies and if the weather was good, a ride to the back shore on Clay Lewis' (Justin's brother's) ATV to "smell the ocean and check on things" and back home to work crossword puzzles. In the evening they watched VHS movies rented from the store. (Savannah watched, Ev dozed.)

It wasn't long before even that was too much. First the rides to the back shore stopped, then trips to Loretta's became fewer. When Ev stopped going altogether the islanders migrated one by one to Ev's cottage. Lilly would make coffee and encourage Savannah to "get some air" which she did. They would all sit at the kitchen table and argue about the newest lobstering restrictions, what to do about the overpopulation of deer on the island, or Claude Beaumarchais' new boat. Subjects that had been mined and autopsied over the years were disinterred and revisited with great relish. Sometimes Ev would make his way to the couch and fall asleep. No one seemed to mind.

Some days the very young Congregational minister, Rev. Roan Rayland, would come by and listen, wide-eyed the whole time. He often left the cottage without addressing his mission of comforting and blessing his flock but super inspired with exciting ideas and lessons for sermons to come.

Lilly more or less conscripted Juliette Durand to help Ev with his medications. She had been a nurse in Portland and now on the island, married to a lobsterman, she became the island's go-to person for emergencies and she was every young mother's greatest resource. Juliette flirted and cajoled Ev into compliance for the things he didn't want to do, like adding a stool softener to his already impressive pill box and insisting he drink more fluids. Savannah could see that Ev enjoyed the banter.

Inevitably, the weather changed to the cold damp and fog of late autumn. Walking was more treacherous, one's footing was less sure on the slippery rocks and roots. Ice crystals would form during the night and melt during the day if the sun deigned to come out, which was rare.

Weather conditions did little to slow down the visitors to Ev Spear's cottage, but the routines inside did change. Ev no longer sat in his kitchen chair but went straight to the couch. Savannah didn't want to hover, but she did as he was more and more unsteady when he walked. And he slept even more than before. Still the sounds that emanated from the cottage, at times, sounded like a raucous party.

*So different from when her mother died five years earlier,* Savannah thought. Her mother (Ev's daughter) was in a hospital. Everything was hushed and antiseptic. Savannah and Ev had spent time in various waiting rooms drinking bad coffee and not knowing what to say to each other.

Sometimes Lilly would come to the cottage in the evening with a bottle of Four Roses and she and Savannah would talk quietly. Lilly had stories. Stories about Ev, stories about the island, stories about the sea. Sometimes she listened more than she spoke. Savannah was beginning to understand why her grandfather liked Lilly.

As the days ticked by, Savannah marveled at the resilience of the human spirit. *As things changed, there would be shock and grief. Then you adjust,* Savannah thought. The diagnosis, the changes in routine, becoming bedridden. Those things would quickly become the new norm. Life is life and you are grateful for any shred that remains.

The first dusting of snow made the island all the more treacherous. When Lilly came that morning Savannah marveled at her footwear. Boots with tufts of fur popping out the top and through the laces, and stainless steel cleats harnessed to the soles. "I bet you don't see these much in Boston," Lilly laughed. "Go for your walk."

Savannah's "runs" had become careful slow walks. To her surprise, they proved to be just as satisfying. The ocean and the wildness were soothing in their own right and some days she wanted the walks to go on forever. Today was one

**Georgette Carignan**
**Limerick, ME**

of those days.

On her return she saw it all in Lilly's face. Lilly said nothing but gave her a hug. "He was a very private man. He chose his time," she said.

Savannah went to his room. He was gone. She could see it and feel it. Still, she felt for his pulse. She didn't trust herself as her heart was beating so wildly she was afraid that she would feel her own pulse in her fingertips. But she didn't.

"Oh Grandpa," she breathed. Her brain emptied completely and the words "Oh, Grandpa" reverberated and bounced around over and over again in the empty space that was the inside of her skull.

After a time, Lilly came in. They sat together in silence, each trying to absorb this new reality.

"What now?" Savannah asked.

Lilly slowly straightened her back and looked at Savannah, "We'll figure it out." Lilly patted Savannah's hand and went into the kitchen. Savannah followed like a lost puppy.

Lilly called Juliette who came immediately. Juliette organized some supplies and said to the women that she was going to clean him up. Lilly went with her to help. When they were done, Savannah went in. Everything was orderly, Ev was neat and clean and appeared peaceful and still very dead. Savannah marveled that even in his weakened state he could be so much a presence, and just moments later, be so completely and thoroughly gone.

Justin Lewis let himself in and quietly made his way to the bedroom. He nodded to the women and stood over Ev's bed and said a silent prayer.

"Justin, you're a good boy," Lilly said. He smiled at the "boy" remark and winked at Savannah. She smiled back.

"The boat's ready when you need it," he said.

Savannah looked panicked. *Are we really going to do this? Just dump him overboard?*

Lilly saw Savannah's look of horror, "Honey, Justin can

just as easily take him to Stonington and we can arrange for the funeral parlor to pick him up at the dock... if that's what you want." She paused for Savannah to take it in. "But you know it's not what *he* wanted."

Savannah nodded trying to get a grip on what she had promised Ev on a beautiful autumn day in October and now looked out the window at the grayness and fog. *What was it that Ev would say? "Always be true to your word." He had always put a lot of stock in honest follow through,* she thought.

Savannah turned back to Justin, "In the morning," she said.

Loretta had let herself into the kitchen with a big plate of donuts. Rev. Roan came in shortly after and went straight to Savannah and hugged her. Then to Lilly. Then he went into the bedroom.

As the afternoon wore on coffee became coffee and whiskey, and then the coffee was tossed out altogether. People she had never seen before came to the cottage, she didn't know there were that many people on the island. Casseroles and cakes appeared. Savannah heard the scrape of a snow shovel on the steps and paths around the cottage. Maddy Wilkes came via Clay Lewis' ATV with her walker tied to the back. Savannah smiled, even the island's resident curmudgeon came to pay her respects to Ev. She remembered Ev laughing, saying he liked her as they were the same age and she was feisty, "like me." Savannah did not think they were alike at all, still she had to give Maddy credit for coming. It couldn't have been easy. Clay escorted her into the bedroom where they stayed for a few minutes. When they came out she nodded at Savannah, and Savannah saw, in her eyes, a genuine sadness. Maddy patted Lilly's hand and Clay helped her back on the ATV and home again.

Savannah dozed in the big chair, Lilly slept in the rocker and the dawn came all too quickly. Justin had come in and out several times during the night. He shook Savannah's shoulder, "We should get going," he said.

"Yes, yes..." she said even though her brain was saying no, no. Lilly was awake and stretching the creaks out of her joints.

The three went into the bedroom. Ev was now in a lime green plastic toboggan. He was swaddled in bed linens and secured to the toboggan with rope. Only his face was exposed. Savannah considered herself pragmatic even hard-nosed but this made her wince. She had a moment of longing for sprays of gladioli, piped in organ music, and cadavers over made-up to look like people sleeping.

She tapped on the sled and looked at Justin. "It belonged to Juliette's kids. We thought it would work for an impromptu burial at sea." Smiles creeped onto each of their faces.

Justin became serious and looked at Savannah, "Ev and I talked a few months back. He knew what he wanted and he had faith you were up for it."

Savannah just moaned a little and couldn't look away from Ev's face. She kissed him and said, "Good bye Grandpa, I love you." She covered his face and tucked the blankets in around his head.

Craig was waiting at the door with the ATV. Juliette was there also. They fastened the toboggan to the back and Craig drove slowly, with Savannah, Lilly, Justin and Juliette following on foot behind him. Though it wasn't far to the dock, it was extremely slow going. Halfway there Savannah slipped onto one knee, and the pain made her want to cry. It surprised her that she could feel so much pain in her knee when her heart and soul felt so dead. Lilly was far more sure-footed with her fantasmagorical footwear and a walking stick.

Loretta was sweeping snow off the front steps of the café when they walked past. She nodded and put her hand to her heart. Claude stopped working on his lines and stood at attention and saluted the cortege. Rev. Roan came running down the hill to catch up. It was a slow, arms flailing for balance, kind of run. He fell in step behind the small group.

**Georgette Carignan**
**Limerick, ME**

Jimmy, the store owner, stepped out onto the steps, lit a cigarette and watched intently acknowledging them with a nod. His wife, Freda, rushed out with a Christmas wreath and gave it to Savannah who looked puzzled. "To mark the spot. I didn't have time to make a real funeral one."

"Thank you," she said, still a little confused.

Once under way, Justin broke out his large thermos of coffee. He poured a cup for each one. Predictably, it was well-braced with whiskey. Savannah smiled into the cup. Normally she would tick off all the reasons why this was absolutely not a good idea, but right now she was simply grateful for the warmth it provided.

Savannah leaned into Justin, pulling his shoulder down so her lips were close to his ear. "Is this legal?" she whispered. His shrug confirmed what she already knew. He squinted at the huge expanse of ocean all around them, "So keep a look out, just in case. You know, for the funeral police."

After an hour, Justin stopped the boat, lowered the anchor and turned to Savannah. No words were needed. The toboggan had been weighted with ballast stones and was heavy. Everyone grabbed a hold and hoisted the sled with Everett in it onto the rail and let it slide into the dark water, feet first. It disappeared from view almost immediately.

Savannah was shocked. Then she remembered the wreath. She retrieved it from the bench and quickly threw it into the water. To her relief it floated. Lilly pulled out a framed picture of Ev when he was seventeen in his Navy uniform. Savannah hadn't seen that picture in years. Lilly threw it in the vicinity of the wreath and blew a kiss.

Rev. Roan looking especially pale, pulled out a Bible and started reciting Psalm Twenty Three. Shoulders touching, they all stared into the water. The wreath bounced and sparkled with glitter and plastic snowflakes and a waving, chubby cheeked Santa Claus. And for a few moments, a bright, smiling seventeen year old sailor smiled up at them.

**Carol Altieri**
**Madison, CT**

## Germany's Black Forest/Shinrin-yoku*

*Trees are poems that the earth writes upon the sky.*
**—Khalil Gibran**

I love taking the hike through Germany's Black Forest,
a haven where memories of holidays and childhood
emerge from a repository of traditions and time.

Drunk with the legends, I know this forest
is sacred as if a god descended
on a mountain of the highest fir trees.

A series of groves encloses me in silvery-sheen
fir foliage. Fairies, gnomes, trolls
and witches conjure here as the Grimm brothers
found their inspiration for fairy tales: *Hansel and Gretel,*
*Little Red Riding Hood,* and *Rapunzel.*

When I gaze up at the canopy of dense fir trees,
the sky appears like a stream of tributaries
winding through the forest
and the spicy, resinous fragrance fills the air.

The forest birds, woodpeckers, owls and warblers
love this place too with its centuries'—old fir trees
for building nests. I hear their quirky calls
as they perch overhead.
Their eyes pinned to the nests they build.

The forest hums with life.
Farmers raise hams and cooks bake cakes.
German farm houses and castles flourish

**Carol Altieri**
**Madison, CT**

where hard working craftsmen
create cuckoo clocks that rhythmically sing.

*Shinrin-yoku is the Japanese practice to contemplate the full atmosphere and feel the shadowy surroundings with all my senses.

***

**Bob Whitmire**
**Round Pond, ME**

## Transit to Reykjavik

Icelandair 767 bores through frigid
air at 35,000 feet, three-quarter moon
staring back at us from beyond
the right wing tip. It looks like we
are all even-steven on the same level,
a faint trace of moongloss lying soft
across a choppy, unbroken sea of clouds.

We ascended out of rain in Boston;
we will descend into rain in Reykjavik,
but for this moment we're weightless,
smooth, clear like blown crystal
under the attentive eye
of the waning gibbous moon
and I forget how uncomfortable it is
to be folded into space
hardly fit for a mid-sized dog.

**Thomas Peter Bennett**
**Silver Spring, MD**

## A Request

In the chair, casting an anxious glance
        at the wall clock,
while I wait for the dentist...

Yes, the lamb chop was delicious, until—
        *Crack*—a sudden pain...
I knew I'd fractured an old, faithful molar.
        Now, I await its extraction...

The dentist arrives
        and greets me politely.
"This may sting,"
        he cautions me,
as he twice punctures the gum
        near my broken tooth.

"Please relax," he adds.
        "The anesthesia will take several minutes to work."
I do, and it does,
        as the lower left part
of my jaw magically disappears.

His assistant supplies
        him with
tools seriatim as he begins his work.

"Please raise your left hand if you feel any pain,"
        he tells me.
Thankfully, there is no need!

**Thomas Peter Bennett**
**Silver Spring, MD**

My eyes follow the minute hand of the wall clock
        as it completes a quarter turn
while his excavation takes place.

"At last," he announces, "it's out!"
        He shows me the bloody and broken tooth.

On my pocket notepad, I write a message
        and hold it up for him to see.
"Please save it—
        the tooth fairy still visits."

***

**Elmae Passineau**
**Weston, WI**

## Bending the Law

My first gin and sour,
  when I was twenty
  and one year shy of legality,
  was in the company of a policeman,
  my boyfriend that year
The bar owner never questioned
  his request—
  assuming perhaps that an officer of the law
  would keep the law
So, ten months later,
  he was mightily surprised
  when we celebrated at his bar
  my twenty-first birthday

## *GOOSE RIVER ANTHOLOGY, 2020*

We seek selections of fine poetry, essays, and short stories (3,000 words or less) for the 18th annual *Goose River Anthology, 2020.* The book will be beautifully produced with full color cover and full color dust jacket for hard covers.

You may submit even if you have been published before in a previous edition of the *Goose River Anthology.* We retain one-time publishing rights. All rights revert back to the author after publication. You may submit as many pieces as you like.

**EARN CASH ROYALTIES.** Author will receive a 10% royalty on all sales that he or she generates.

There is no purchase required and nothing is required of the author for publication. Deadline for submissions is April 30, 2020. Publication will be in the fall of 2020 (they make great Christmas gifts). Guidelines are as follows:

- Submit clean, typed copy by snail mail—**mandatory**
- Email a Word, rtf, or PDF file to us (if possible)
- Reading fee: $1.00 per page
- Do not put two poems on the same page
- Essays and short stories **must be** double-spaced
- **SASE (#10 or larger) for notification** (one forever stamp) plus additional postage for possible return of submission if desired.
- Author's name & address at top of each page of paper copy and first page of emailed copies.

Submit to:
*Goose River Anthology, 2020*
3400 Friendship Road
Waldoboro, ME 04572-6337
E mail: gooseriverpress@roadrunner.com
www.gooseriverpress.com

CPSIA information can be obtained
at www.ICGtesting.com
Printed in the USA
BVHW030143260220
573314BV00005B/10/J

9 781597 132084